TIGER AT BAY

A Sixties Mystery

BERNARD KNIGHT

First published in Great Britain by Robert Hale Ltd 1970
This edition published by Accent Press 2016

ISBN 9781910939918

The story contained within this book is a work of fiction. Names and characters are the product of the author's imagination and any resemblance to actual persons, living or dead, is entirely coincidental.

For

HUW KNIGHT

the most important inhabitant of the city in which the action of this book takes place

Author's note

The Sixties Mysteries is a series of reissues of my early crime stories, the first of which was originally published in 1963. Looking back now, it is evident how criminal investigation has changed over the last half-century. Though basic police procedure is broadly the same, in these pages you will find no Crime Scene Managers or Crown Prosecution Service, no DNA, CSI, PACE, nor any of the other acronyms beloved of modern novels and television. These were the days when detectives still wore belted raincoats and trilby hats. There was no Health and Safety to plague us and the police smoked and drank tea alongside the post-mortem table!

Modern juries are now more interested in the reports of the forensic laboratory than in the diligent labours of the humble detective, though it is still the latter that solves most serious crimes. This is not to by any means belittle the enormous advances made in forensic science in recent years, but to serve as a reminder that the old murder teams did a pretty good job based simply on experience and dogged investigation.

Bernard Knight
2015

Chapter One

The Glendower Arms was set a few feet lower than the pavement and three steps led down to the uninviting entrance of the saloon bar. The steps were worn smooth by three generations of thirsty workmen. The night was heavy with mist and the lamp above the door had gone out. Looking back on it, Iago Price reckoned that he had a good excuse for falling down the steps. With a muffled yell, he skidded over the slippery treads and cannoned into the varnished door. The latch gave way and he fell ignominiously onto his hands and knees just inside.

'You're useless,' said his secretary caustically. 'Now shut the door, I don't want all that fog down my throat.'

She twisted haughtily on her stool and carried on talking in her strong Cardiff accent to the landlord, who had been gazing at Iago's dramatic entry in silent admiration.

Price hauled himself to his feet and slammed the door. He brushed down his pseudo-officer's greatcoat with one hand, then pressed a dent from his bowler before advancing on the bar.

Lewis Evans, the licensee, sighed. 'Can't you never do nothing right, Iago? Anything within half a mile and you'll fall over it.'

Price's mousy moustache bristled. 'That's enough, both of you. I'm not going to take the needle from a publican – nor an employee!'

He wasn't being funny, but the girl giggled and the man behind the bar smiled pityingly.

'Cut it out, Iago, don't come the big city businessman

with me. Have you paid this month's rent on your office yet?' he asked cynically.

Iago's sallow face reddened slightly. 'Just shut up, Lewis, and give me a whisky.'

Lewis Evans feigned surprise.

'Spirits, eh! Had a Premium Bond up?' He turned to get the drink and Iago shrugged off his overcoat. Without it, he looked half the size, a thin, weedy young man with a slight stoop. His head was too big for his neck and was topped by thin fair hair that matched his feeble moustache. With his perpetually mournful expression, he looked just what he was – one of nature's born losers.

It was shortly after opening time on a filthy December night and the only other patron was a deaf old man in the corner, oblivious to everything except his pint and his copy of *Sporting Life*. The girl ignored Iago as he sat down next to her and looked around the bar. He switched on a leering smile and touched his knee against hers. She instantly moved it away, without looking up from manicuring her nails.

'What'll you have, Dilys?' he fawned.

Her eyes swivelled round and the arched eyebrows rose in sarcastic enquiry. 'Well I never! You robbed a bank or something?'

The few score hairs of his moustache tried to bristle.

'Look, don't be so damn clever – do you want a drink or not?'

She softened a little, the message that Iago was being pushed a bit far getting through even her thick skin.

'Oh, ta, then. Lewis, what's the most expensive drink you got?'

'Treble vodka and brandy, love.'

'No, I'll just have a gin and lime, I think.'

'Right, one Maiden's Ruin coming up. That's seven and thruppence, Mr Price. And I hope you got it!'

Iago sullenly laid a pound note on the bar. 'That's

better!' he muttered.

'What is?' asked the landlord, a dark, thickset Celt whose black eyebrows met in the middle.

'Calling me *Mister* Price.'

Dilys Thomas kicked him hard on the ankle. 'What's the matter with you tonight? All this lord of the manor stuff. And you haven't tried to make a proper pass at me since elevenses You sickening for something?'

Iago looked at her, then dipped a hand into his breast pocket. He passed over a folded piece of paper. Dilys smoothed it out on the bar with her scarlet-tipped fingers. Her eyebrows made another excursion up her forehead, this time in genuine surprise.

'A cheque for forty-two quid!'

Iago pointed with pride to the printed account-holder's name. 'David Powell Ltd! The big department store opposite the castle.' Her big brown eyes gave him a reluctant look of admiration.

'This is the biggest cheque we've ever had. What you done, sold 'em your car? Forty-two pound is just about what it's worth.'

Pulling his leg in a semi-serious way had become such a habit that Dilys was unable to stop, even when she felt such reflected pride in the arrival of some long-overdue success.

Iago carefully folded the paper and put it away.

'This could be a regular contract, if I handle it right,' he said proudly. 'Investigating hire purchase applicants. They've had such a lot of dead ducks lately that they're getting worried about who they flog their washing machines to.'

Dilys sniffed disdainfully.

'The money's welcome, God knows. But it's a bit dull, eh? I thought Powell's were going to ask you to catch a blackmailer or an embezzler.'

Iago sipped his whisky before answering. He didn't

really care for the stuff – it burned his mouth and the smell reminded him of being sick after parties at college, but it seemed more the stuff for up-and-coming 'private eyes' than mere beer.

Things were looking up, much to his surprise. He had had a good run of divorce cases lately, enough to pay his one and only employee and almost cover the rent. The work was grim and mainly consisted of following furtive co-respondents around on Cardiff Corporation buses, or walking endlessly up and down in the freezing cold outside suburban houses, waiting for the guilty party to emerge from their love-nests. It paid quite well and with this windfall of hire purchase status enquiries, the ebbing tide of financial solvency seemed on the turn.

'I think we're on the way, Dilys!' He said this so long after she had last spoken that she had no idea what he was talking about.

'Whaddya say?' she snapped.

Iago sighed. Dilys was a marvellous girl, if hardly a lady. When she opened her mouth, she put her foot in it.

'I said, we're going to make the grade as a detective agency. The tide has turned, Dilys love.'

'Don't "love" me,' she said automatically. 'You want to do something about your name, then.'

'Yes, bloody daft, that is,' cut in Lewis Evans, who had just come back from the cellar.

Iago Price scowled. He was sick of being ribbed about the nameplate fixed outside his seedy office up the road. This read, 'I. PRICE – CONFIDENTIAL ENQUIRIES.' He had not spotted the horrible pun on his name until too late, in spite of being saddled with it for the past thirty years.

'I'm going to form a limited company soon,' he muttered. 'Change it to "DETECTION WALES LTD." or something snappy like that.' For the next few moments, he and his secretary sipped their drinks in silence.

Dilys was thinking of the clumsy strength of the hairy Arts student she had grappled with after a dance the previous night. Iago was dividing his attention between daydreams about his nice new cheque and daydreams about the wide expanse of smooth thigh that Dilys was showing as her miniskirt was rucked up on the high bar stool. Lost in these higher thoughts, they both failed to notice a new arrival in the bar. A man came in and began making furtive signs to the landlord. Lewis went over to him.

'Is that Mr Price – Mr Iago Price?' hissed the newcomer.

Lewis nodded, his black hair flopping over his face.

'That's him!' He turned and bellowed down the bar, 'Customer here for you, Iago. Blackmail or divorce, by the looks of him.'

The man turned as white as a sheet so Lewis Evans picked up Iago's drink and slammed it down next to the stranger. 'Sit there, Mr Price … have a consultation on the house!'

The self-appointed detective glared at the barman, then moved down the bar and murmured some apology to the newcomer, a well-built man of about fifty. He was quite well-dressed but had a vaguely neglected look about him, like a strong plant starting to go to seed. His worried look was characteristic of most of Iago's clients.

'Were you looking for me, sir?' asked Iago, in his most cultured voice, the only asset he had acquired from eight years in an obscure English public school.

The other man bobbed his head, the fleshy pouches under his eyes wobbling. 'I went to your office and they said next door that you would be here.'

His voice tailed off and he looked anxiously around the saloon bar.

The landlord caught the glance and chipped in cheerfully. 'Carry on, mate … Gorgeous Gussie here is Mr

Price's confidential secretary. And don't worry about Ted over there, he's as deaf as a post.' He waved airily to the corner, where the cloth-capped figure was now fast asleep, his *Sporting Life* dropped on the senile spaniel who lay drooling at his feet.

Iago leaned nearer.

'Did you want to see me professionally?' He said this last word with the reverence of an archbishop uttering the most awesome part of his liturgy.

The man nodded again. 'I must see you! I've made my mind up and I've got to get it over with.'

The words just reached Dilys and she sighed. She was a sentimental girl under her tough crust and the thought that another husband had just discovered that his wife was tumbling with the insurance man depressed her. Still, it might pay the electricity bill.

'Can you tell me what it's about?' Iago Price had come to the same conclusion as his secretary and was now using his consultant psychiatrist's voice.

The stranger's prominent blue eyes roved around in anguish. 'Not here. Can we go to your office?'

Iago sighed internally, but smiled his assent and stood up. He knocked his stool over and dropped his overcoat, but eventually got as far as the door with the prospective client.

As he held the door for the other to go out into the fog, Iago waved to Dilys. 'I won't be long, then I'll come back and take you for a meal or something.'

She poked her pointed tongue at him. Iago scowled and let the door swing shut onto his ankle, but otherwise they reached his office without any further disaster.

'Up these stairs, please,' he said politely. They had reached a dirty door just around the corner from the Hayes Bridge Road. The side street was poorly lit and in the heavy mist, only the loom of the warehouses could be seen.

‘I. PRICE – CONFIDENTIAL ENQUIRIES’ was housed in a single room above a greengrocer’s shop. Though the entrance was in the side street, the windows of the office were on the first floor facing the main road which joined Cardiff’s shopping centre with the dock area. It was something of a no-man’s land, where the modern brightness of the city centre clashed with the seedy legacy of the world’s greatest coal port. At present, the down-at-heel element was winning, though its victory was going to be short-lived. The area was going to be vaporized by the City Council and rebuilt into hygienic anonymity.

None of this passed through Iago’s mind as he trudged up the splintered, uncarpeted staircase. He was wondering how much he could screw out of this punter for all the legwork necessary to prove infidelity.

At the top, he fumbled for his keys, dropped them and scrabbled in the dark to find them on the dirty floor.

‘Isn’t there a light?’ asked the client, rather sourly.

‘The kids keep pinching the bulb. We’ve given up putting them in,’ grunted Iago, feeling for the keyhole like a drunk after a night’s binge. He got in at last and turned the light on. The office was revealed in all the brilliance of a 40-watt bulb.

The one large room was divided by a crude plaster-board partition, leaving one third for Dilys’s desk and the second-hand typewriter. A few hard chairs were ranged optimistically around for waiting customers.

Iago led the way through to the inner office, where the spartan furnishing consisted of another desk, two chairs and a filing cabinet.

The lower half of the sash window had been whitewashed in lieu of curtains and the naked bulb threw an unkind glare on the flaking plaster of the walls and ceiling.

The enquiry agent waved his client to a chair and sat himself behind the desk.

‘If I could have your name, then we can start a file.’ He leaned sympathetically across the blotter.

‘Summers – Michael Summers. I live in Rhiwbina.’ He gave Iago an address on the north side of the city and the younger man dutifully noted it down on the back of a postcard.

Iago looked up encouragingly at Summers, but he seemed to have dried up.

‘Er, some domestic worry, perhaps?’ the detective prompted.

Summers nodded dolefully, but still said nothing.

‘Er … a worry over a lady, eh?’ suggested Price delicately.

The client suddenly became more communicative. He leant forward confidentially.

‘Look, I haven’t come about a divorce, if that’s what you’re after. More like trying to avoid one, in fact!’

He ran a hand through his grey hair in a gesture of despair. ‘I’m in a hell of a spot, Mr Price. I should go to the police, but I daren’t.’

Iago saw the imagined cheque disappearing into the distance. The mention of police depressed him, not because he had any reason to dislike them, but a year’s experience in the ‘private eye trade’ had taught him that when the police came in, profit usually went out.

He began rolling his ballpoint between his fingers and tried to give a Perry Mason look from under lowered eyebrows.

‘I’m not sure that I can help you, Mr Summers, if this is a police matter.’

The pouchy-faced man shook his head wearily.

‘It isn’t – yet. I came to you with the hope of stopping it becoming one.’

Iago stole a crafty look at his watch. If this was going to be a wash-out, he would rather be back at the pub. Twelve months of continuous brush-off from Dilys had still not convinced him that he would never make the grade with her. If he could get back there before her latest lover turned up, she might have some miraculous change of heart.

Before he could think up some excuse, Summers put both hands on the desk and looked appealingly at Iago. 'I'm desperate, Mr Price, I tell you. I'm in the same trade as you, in a manner of speaking, but this has me beat. I've even thought of doing myself in …

He ended on a strangled sob and Iago, always a sucker for the hard-luck sell, muttered at him to carry on.

'It's like this – I'm a security officer for the Celtic Bank,' began Summers. 'It's not one of the Big Five, but it's got a lot of branches in the city.' He dropped his voice so that even Iago's wing-like ears had a job to pick up his words.

'About a month ago, I got mixed up with a girl. Looking back, of course it was a put-up job. This woman, Betty, came to work in the Head Office as a cleaner and tea-girl. She was always giving me big smiles and seemed to be bumping into me every time I went into the pub next door.'

He looked up and there was bitterness in his face. 'Old fool that I was – flattered by her, I suppose. She made me feel that perhaps I wasn't too old after all.'

Iago, who was too easily embarrassed to be a good enquiry agent, couldn't see where all this was leading. He stopped writing on his postcard and began drawing spiral doodles.

'One thing led to another, see. I had plenty of opportunity. I had to go out most evenings, visiting branches to check security.'

Summers fiddled with his collar. 'She had a flat in Richmond Road, said she was divorced. We used to have fun of an evening. I'd take a bottle in and we'd have a good laugh and that …'

His voice tailed off and left Iago wondering what exactly 'that' referred to.

Summers got himself back in gear. 'I don't remember all I talked about. We said so much and I had quite a drop to drink some nights. Once, she betted me in fun, so I thought, that I couldn't remember all the names of the branch managers. I said I could and wrote them all down on a scrap of paper. Didn't matter a damn – no secret about it. We just had a good laugh.'

Iago stopped doodling. Though he was a long way down the queue when they handed out brains, it was obvious even to him where all this was leading.

'Yesterday, a chap came to see me at work. A real fly boy, "villain" written all over him. He showed me a photo.' Summers swallowed and gripped the edge of the desk.

Iago cleared his throat in heightened embarrassment.

'The sort we read about in these spy books?' he ventured helpfully.

Summers shook his head vehemently. 'Just showed our heads together in bed – but to think that that bloody yob must have been hiding in the flat with a camera!'

'What was his pitch?' asked Iago.

'He said he had a piece of paper with all the managers' names in my writing. He showed it to me but alongside each name, somebody had typed the address of the branch and the name of the counter staff. This character said that it could be proved that it had been typed on one of the machines at Head Office – obviously Betty had done it when she was cleaning.'

Iago scratched his head with the blunt end of the pen. He could not see where he was supposed to come into the story.

'Blackmail – but what for?'

'He wanted the security arrangements in three of the branches. Types of safe, alarm circuits, watchmen arrangements, the lot. He still wants them – by tomorrow, otherwise he says he'll send the photo and the list to the area manager of Celtic – and a copy of the photo to my wife.'

Summers did a bit more frenzied hair-raking with his fingers.

'It'll finish me either way. If I don't do what he says. I'll lose my job, pension – the lot! And as for my wife ... Christ! She's not the type to forgive and forget.'

Iago massaged his wilting moustache. 'This list ... it's nothing, as far as blackmail goes. Anybody could get the names of the managers. And the names of the counter staff are stuck up on their tills – anyone going in for bobs for the gas meter could get those!'

The security man stuck his neck out almost defiantly.

'I know ... but would you risk it, with that photo? I'm supposed to be in charge of security! The bank would have to heave me out on my ear, they could never trust me after this, even though I've committed no criminal offence. We're like doctors and clergymen, we're vulnerable in our game. If there's smoke, it doesn't matter about there being no fire!'

Iago rocked back on his chair. 'Then you'll have to go to the police.'

Summers slapped his big hand on the desk. 'I can't. I know quite a few of the chaps there, they couldn't do a thing without going to the bank, and that'd be the same as my telling this yob to get stuffed. They've got me over a barrel!'

Iago had to agree with him. Although, as blackmail, it was an anaemic effort, in practice it was as effective as if the security man had been caught at a black magic orgy with the Celtic safe combinations tattooed across his backside.

'But why come to me – I can't undo what's been done, can I?'

Summers wagged his head from side to side. 'I want to know who they are,' he said doggedly. 'I want you to tail this chap tomorrow, find out where he comes from and who he associates with. You should be able to do that blindfold, after all those divorce jobs.'

Iago pondered for a moment. Although the set-up didn't appeal to him one bit, he was reluctant to pass up a simple bloodhound job that should last only an hour or two. And this chap Summers was a security officer, perhaps in a position to recommend more business – if he survived his present sticky predicament.

'Well, I suppose I can … but what good will it do you? They'll have you over the same barrel once you give them any proper information.'

Summers shrugged helplessly. 'What else can I do? I want time to think out some action. If you can find out who these bastards are, maybe I can work around to some unofficial word with the pals I have in the police. I just don't know, but I've got to buy some time. This was only sprung on me today.'

Iago got up and looked at his watch. *She'll have gone by now*, he thought, so he sat down again.

'What about the woman – Betty, wasn't it? What happened to her?

Summers turned up his palms. 'Vanished! Didn't come to work today. I went around the flat, she'd done a flit. It was only a furnished place, rented by the week.'

The private detective had another scratch at his head with the ballpoint. 'So where do I pick up this fellow tomorrow?'

'I'm meeting him in the Red Dragon in Queen Street at one thirty. You can't miss him, he's a tall, greasy- haired yob with long black sideboards. Looks like a Soho mobster, except that he's got a Rhondda accent you can cut with a knife!'

Iago turned his card over and scribbled on it. 'Only a

one-day job. That'll be five guineas and expenses.'

Summers nodded and hauled himself to his feet, looking ten years more than his age.

'Where will I see you?' he muttered.

'In the pub over the road, same time tomorrow evening,' said Iago.

They went down to the foggy dampness of the street and the bank man trudged away in the direction of the city centre. Iago stumbled over the kerb and set off for the Glendower Arms, in the faint hope that Dilys might still be there.

Chapter Two

Iago Price sat with Dilys at the bar of the Red Dragon and tried to make his one lager last out for the whole operation. Expenses didn't include the cost of his beer and he didn't like drinking at lunchtime, it made him sleepy.

As he kept one eye on Summers, who was hunched in a corner opposite, Iago reflected that most of an enquiry agent's time seemed to be spent either in public houses, telephone boxes or staring into shop windows. He thought sometimes with nostalgia of his last job, a 'con-man'-type salesman in a cheap furniture store. Though less glamorous-sounding than being a 'private detective', at least one stayed in a warm shop and could sit down on the goods – if you could find any strong enough to support you.

His secretary burst in on his reverie. 'If we stay much longer, you're going to have to buy me another drink,' she complained. Her voice jarred on him, but as soon as he turned and looked at the girl, he was lost again. She was slim, she was blonde, she was lovely. Iago almost slobbered mentally as his eyes soaked her up. He was not vain, but he often wondered why a chap of at least average appearance, such as himself, should so consistently get the brush-off from her.

'What about it then?' she snapped, tapping the foot of her empty glass impatiently on the bar. Her own thoughts were simple and uncomplicated, as she could think of only one topic at a time. There was a direct line from her mind to her tongue and she usually spoke with disconcerting frankness.

At the moment, her grey matter was concerning itself with getting another drink, but Iago was saved by the bell. Summers' expected blackmailer was over half an hour late, but suddenly the bank man made a warning jerk of his head.

A moment later, a young man with an insolent face and a shock of greasy black curls dropped on to the chair next to Summers.

He was over six feet tall and had a coarsely handsome face. His colouring, swarthy skin and fleshy lips suggested Italian or even gypsy blood, though unbeknown to Iago his family had in fact lived for generations in the Glamorgan valleys.

'That the feller?' hissed Dilys, switching her mind to her favourite channel – men.

Iago nodded covertly. 'Don't go staring at him. Looks the part, doesn't he? Fancy being his gun moll?'

The blonde sniffed airily.

'Look at the way he dresses. Five years out of date, those trousers. Bet he still does the Twist,' she said contemptuously. 'Smashing lips, though,' she added rather wistfully.

The newcomer was leaning over a sullen Summers, talking rapidly. The security officer finally produced a folded slip of paper and handed it over with every appearance of reluctance, though he told Iago that the information would be next to useless, as he was having the security arrangements altered at once.

The spiv-like character flashed a face-splitting grin and patted Summers on the shoulder. Then he swaggered out of the bar without stopping for a drink.

Price took the opportunity to lay his hand on Dilys' nylon-covered knee in a dramatic gesture of farewell. 'This is my cue, honey!' he hissed.

She pinched the back of his hand viciously with her talons and he hastily took his hand away.

'What are you today – The Saint, The Baron, or the Man from U.N.C.L.E?' she asked sarcastically, as he stumbled from his stool to follow the greasy-haired man.

Though the pavements of the main street were crowded, Iago's quarry stood a head higher than most and he was able to follow him without difficulty to a bus stop a hundred yards away. Iago slunk into a shop doorway and waited for three people to join the queue before adding himself to the end.

A bus came and Greasy-Hair stayed where he was. All the other people got aboard and Iago found himself in the embarrassing position of being shoulder to shoulder with the man he was following. It was thankfully short-lived, as another bus came almost at once. The man jumped on and went upstairs, so Iago sat next to the platform on the lower deck.

When the conductor came, he realized he had no idea where the bus was going. 'Terminus, please,' he asked in a moment of obvious inspiration.

It was soon clear where the bus was going. It went back almost to Iago's office, then turned into the one-way system that led to the top of Bute Street.

Fifty years ago, this was one of the most famous – or rather, infamous – highways in the world. Almost a mile long and dead straight, it joined the respectable city centre to the then notorious dockland of Cardiff.

At the height of the prosperity brought by the coal trade, it was a bawdy, bustling sailor-town. The warren of streets leading off Bute Street were known all over the globe as 'Tiger Bay', where no policeman dared wander alone.

Today, as Iago Price watched it through the windows of a bus, it looked pathetic in its death throes. Half the street itself had been pulled down and most of Tiger Bay behind it was being reduced to a fine dust by Corporation bulldozers.

Neat council houses and teetering skyscraper flats were rising phoenix-like from its ashes. Tiger Bay, once a boisterous den of iniquity, was now a building site.

Yet some of the old area still remained, though it was dying. A few streets of old terrace houses hung to survival by their fingertips; some were derelict and roofless, others were still occupied by the children and grandchildren of the wild old days.

As the bus neared the lower end of the famous street, Iago saw more of the old Tiger Bay, battered by Nazi bombs and Welsh builders, but still on its feet, waiting for the final knockout.

Groups of Lascars and black men lounged outside seedy shops and cafes; children of all shades chased around the uneven pavements. Toothless old women with folded arms and fluffy bedroom slippers pugnaciously guarded their doorways.

Iago had known this area for years. His pompous father had been 'something big down the docks' before he retired and Iago had often visited his office as a child and been taken on tours of ships in the great docks.

Full of distant memories, Iago sat almost oblivious of his task as the bus reached the bottom of Bute Street and entered the equally seedy but un-demolished business sector, filled with shipping offices, ship stores and all the administrative wilderness of those who go down to the sea in ships.

His nostalgia was rudely broken by the sound of large feet clattering on the stairs and the sight of Greasy-Hair suddenly jumping off as the vehicle slowed down at the traffic lights at the James Street crossroads.

Iago leapt up, but the lights had changed and the bus accelerated across.

'Where's the next stop?' he gabbled at the conductor.

The busman shifted his gum from port to starboard and jerked a thumb.

'Ere it is, mate.'

The bus squealed to a halt and Iago fled back to the intersection. Looking frantically about, he sighed with relief when he saw the black, curly head bobbing above the other pedestrians on the other side of the road. He trotted after him and followed for a short distance back up the lower end of Bute Street in the direction they had come. Then the blackmailer turned abruptly off the pavement into a shop doorway and vanished.

Iago slowed down and began to carry out the routine recommended in his Private Eye's Manual. He had sent to New York for this, a paperback 'Teach Yourself Detection' course, complete with plastic badge, magnifying glass and a certificate of enrolment in the New World Academy of Detection!

He walked across the road and nonchalantly gave the premises the once-over from the corner of his eye as he passed.

It was the centre shop of an old three-storey terrace, being flanked by a nautical instrument dealer on one side and the empty premises of a bankrupt grocer on the other. The place that Greasy had entered was actually a cafe. It had once been painted green and over the front was a spidery neon sign tracing out 'Cairo Restaurant'.

The window to one side of the door was obscured by grimy net curtains and over the fanlight of the door was another neon sign in the shape of a star and crescent moon.

Following Rules Two and Three in his book, Iago walked on another fifty yards, crossed over the road and walked back on the side of the cafe. At close range it looked even less inviting, especially as an eating house.

Propped on a bar of the window was a faded and warped card with 'English and Oriental Dishes' at the top. The rest was illegible, but written on the inside of the window glass in whitewash was the legend 'Egg, beans and chips – 2/6d'. Both the 'esses' were backwards.

The New World Academy of Detection left him on his own from here, and Iago wandered uncertainly past the cafe. He stopped to gaze in the windows of the next shop, waiting for inspiration. He stared blankly at the dusty collection of navigational aids that looked as if they had been on display since Drake rounded Cape Horn. He looked at his watch … was two o'clock too late for egg, beans and chips?

He turned, walked boldly to the door of the Cairo Restaurant, and went inside.

His first impression was that he had gone into a disused railway tunnel. As his eyes got used to the winter light that forced its way through the yellowed net curtains, he began to see a double row of tables running down a long, narrow room to a counter at the far end.

The place was empty apart from a little old man with a round Moslem cap and a white apron, who sat near the counter. As the door shut, it gave an anaemic 'ping', and a moment later a fat woman with frizzy hair waddled out from a door at the far end. 'No tea on its own!' she snapped threateningly …

'Egg, beans and chips, please,' retorted Iago, in a tone more fitting to a five-star hotel.

The old woman scowled, banged a bottle of sauce on to the counter, then went duck-footed back into the nether regions.

As he waited for the speciality *de la maison*, Iago looked around him. The tubular steel tables and chairs and the red plastic tablecloths added little to the atmosphere of Cairo, but on the grimy emulsioned walls were a few gaudy panoramas of Egypt. The one immediately above him depicted Port Said apparently in a snowstorm; on looking more closely, he saw that this was due to woodworm having eaten their way through from the back of the picture.

Halfway down the cafe, the underside of a staircase

faced him. The man he had followed from town must have gone either up there or through to the back, he thought.

As the taciturn waitress doled out his meal, he felt no inspiration as to any way of learning more. Chewing through the tasteless chips, he wondered how he was going to justify his five-guinea fee to Summers when they met that evening.

'This feller followed me all the way from the pub. Sitting downstairs now, he is!'

There was an injured note in the voice of the long-haired man. He rejoiced in the name of Joseph Stalin Davies, thanks to his father's political inclinations twenty-eight years earlier.

'Is it the "law", Joe?'

The other man in the second-floor room was busy filing his fingernails and did not look up as he softly asked the question.

Joe Davies shook his head. 'Not even the coppers could be as bad as 'im at trailing somebody! He did about everything bar grabbing hold of my coat tails.'

His companion sat on the window ledge so that the meagre light fell on his manicure operations. He was a very handsome fellow. In his early thirties, he was good-looking in a smooth, almost feline way. Whilst Joe was coarsely attractive in a boxer-cum-pop idol fashion, 'Tiger' Ismail was a genuine throwback to desert tribesmen.

His grandfather had been an Arab stoker who, like so many of his fellows, had settled in Tiger Bay at the turn of the century. He had married a Welsh girl, and his son, who had never set a foot outside South Wales, married a local barmaid.

This last pair had six children, five of whom were indistinguishable from usual Cardiffians, but the sixth was Tiger and he seemed to have inherited a full set of Arabic characteristics. No one knew how he had come by his nickname, as his real one was Lawrence Trefor Ismail, but his cat-like sleekness and his obsession with his immaculate 'talons' had fixed the name so firmly on him that most of his acquaintances had no idea of his real one.

His striking appearance, high intelligence and complete lack of moral sense made a dangerous combination that bordered on the psychopathic. Taken from school at the earliest legal opportunity, he had run with the gangs and soon became a teenage leader.

Though the modern Cardiff dockland is no worse than other areas where delinquency is concerned, Tiger had been deeply involved in what there was of it. After a few salutary appearances in the juvenile court, he became cunning and from then on never managed to take the rap for anything. He despised pointless vandalism and concentrated in those formative days on petty theft and extortion from other youths who had anything to give. When the police or probation officers moved in, it was always one of Tiger's numerous relatives or underlings who took the blame. From seventeen onwards, he was always 'clean' as far as the courts were concerned and this persisted into his adult activities.

The local police division knew a little and suspected a lot more about Tiger's activities, but never again got within a stone's throw of a conviction.

During the last four or five years, even their suspicions died down. Tiger bought the Cairo Restaurant, ostensibly in partnership with two brothers and a sister, and settled down to a respectable life.

Occasionally, the local CID wondered how Tiger managed to support half his family, a new Ford Zodiac and a succession of thirsty girlfriends on the profits from a seedy egg-and-chips dispensary. As he never gave them any trouble, and as even the police informers never had so much as a whisper of any crime in the district being connected with him, he was left in peace.

Tiger was curled up on his window seat now, neatly and expensively dressed in a cream shirt buttoned to the neck, but with no tie. A pair of immaculately creased slacks and soft elastic-sided shoes completed the outfit and emphasised his dark handsomeness.

Even three generations away from the Middle East, a burnous and a camel would have allowed him to slip into Mecca unnoticed, though a careful wave in his jet-black hair clashed slightly with this Bedouin image.

There were those 'down the docks' who said (though not to his face) that Tiger was a bit 'queer'. This was miles from the truth, though he never allowed women to interfere with business. Like with alcohol, Tiger drank when he was thirsty and ignored the girls when he was not.

He looked calmly across at Joe, who was gulping beer.

'So it's not the bogies, then?' he repeated softly.

Joe wiped his mouth with the back of his hand and sneered.

'Nah, this chap don't even look like one. Skinny as 'ell, he is. Looks a proper drip, got a piddling little moustache.'

Tiger gave his gleaming nails a last buffing with a leather pad.

'But it seems that bastard Summers has gone squealing to somebody. Who is it, that's the thing?'

His voice held no accent at all – he avoided both the Welsh lilt and the exaggerated vowels of his native Cardiff.

Joe shrugged. 'Could be a pressman, I suppose, but I've never seen him around before and I know a coupla reporters. I don't know who the 'ell he is, but I'll damn soon find out!'

He banged a fist ominously into the palm of the other hand.

Tiger lifted a hand in an almost languid gesture.

'Go easy, let's dig around a bit first. You say he's actually downstairs?'

Joseph nodded, his oily ringlets bobbing against his scalp.

'Bloody idiot, 'e is! World's biggest amachoor! I knew from the minute he started giving me the eye in the pub that 'e was on to me.'

He scratched his groin as an aid to memory.

'Come to think of it, 'e had a bird with him, a flash bit of stuff. I'd know her again, too – wouldn't mind knocking her off, come to think of it.'

He seemed to be diverted into carnal reverie, but Tiger cut in coldly,

'Tell Florrie to come up a minute – let's see if Auntie can give us a line.'

Again he spoke softly, but Joe jumped up at once and went out. He was Tiger's lieutenant, but knew his place. Cunning, but short on intelligence, Joe was very much the strong-arm man who moved only when Tiger pulled the strings. There were two others in the hub of the gang, but a host of Tiger's family and minor layabouts collected by Joe were on the margin of the several rackets that Tiger carefully manipulated.

Joe soon came back with Florrie, the woman who had served Iago downstairs. A sister of Tiger's mother, she ran the cafe which was a convenient cover for the comings and goings of the people involved with Tiger.

'This chap, Florrie. Ever seen him before?'

His aunt shook her head, the flabby jowls quivering. 'Never! He's no copper, though.' Her speech was thick, suiting her dowdiness and overweight frame, but her little eyes were sharp.

'Think he might be another security bloke from the bank?'

She shrugged her flabby shoulders. 'How would I know? But any firm would be slipping if they took on a twerp like 'im.'

She sank onto the arm of a chair while Tiger uncoiled

himself and padded across the room. In contrast to the scruffy cafe downstairs, Tiger's own quarters were well decorated and furnished. A thick carpet, deep black leather suite and cocktail bar approached the luxurious. On the rest of this second floor were several bedrooms which accommodated the owner and, on occasions, others of the mob.

Tiger paced up and down silently for a few moments, a favourite way of exercising his mind rather than his body. He stopped abruptly and turned to the other two.

'I'll go down the back stairs and have a look at this chap through the serving hatch, see if I know him. You go and chat him up, Florrie, see what you can find out.'

He made for the door, but stopped with his hand on the knob.

'Joe, ring up two of the lads and get them to tail him when he leaves. When he gets home, one of them stays with him, the other belts back here – right?' He held up a hand to show the strong, pointed nails. 'Tell them that if they lose him, I'll mark them to the bone!'

He opened the door and slid away.

Florrie's efforts at pumping Iago Price were no more successful than his own hopes of finding out more about the blackmailers. The fat woman came downstairs in a much more amiable mood than before. When she brought him a cup of tea and took away his dirty plate, she started a conversation which soon led around to asking who he was and where he came from.

Although Iago had no idea that she was pumping him, he stoutly stuck to some non-committal story, following Chapter Six of his American handbook, which told him never to give away gratuitous information.

In turn, however, she stonewalled all his questions about who owned the restaurant and who might be living there. No, she only worked there – started last week, in fact. Didn't know the real owner, but the little chap Ahmed – the one with the round cap – managed the place.

After he had drunk his tea and sat for a few more minutes, Iago was stumped as to his next move. He had no excuse to stay any longer and he wasn't built for any dramatic moves like dashing suddenly up the back stairs to see what went on up above.

He consoled himself with the thought that at least he'd found where Summers' blackmailers hung out. The best thing he could do was to report back to the bank man and let him worry about the next step – not that Iago could see what Summers could possibly do about the situation. Even if the original blackmail would not have stirred up his employers much, the betrayal of their strongroom security would have put Summers right in the mire today.

Iago paid his modest bill and wandered reluctantly out into Bute Street. He looked down towards the bus stop, then momentarily straightened his shoulders.

'To hell with the buses – I'll take a taxi.'

The sweet, if somewhat dilute, taste of success over his hire purchase coup made him feel that no really successful private eye depended on public transport.

A few yards in the opposite direction was a garage with a car hire service. He walked to it and a few moments later was rolling importantly northwards to the city.

Before the car was a hundred yards away, two figures ran up to the little office of the garage.

'Sam, Tiger wants to know where that chap went.' The speaker was a ferrety little man in a peaked cap.

'Hayes Bridge Road! Why?'

The small fellow waved a wad of papers at Sam. 'He dropped this in the caff.' He ran back to a Vauxhall which had just drawn up at the kerb. Together with his companion, a young lad of indeterminate coffee colour, they jumped into the back. The driver, a burly middle-aged man with an acne-scarred complexion, let in the clutch and they tore away up Bute Street after the hire car.

Three minutes later Iago was at his office door As soon as he had vanished inside, the Vauxhall stopped a few yards away and Archie Vaughan, the jockey-like character, hopped out. He waved the car away and turned to inspect the two nameplates outside the seedy entrance. One was Iago's, the other the headquarters of the Omega Clothing Cheque Company. Archie had little doubt which one housed his quarry, but to make sure, he went up to the Clothing Company and made some feeble excuse to enter the office.

A quick look around showed him that no thin, stooped, moustached person was employed there – though the solitary female typist almost qualified for that description.

Back on the street, Vaughan found a phone box within sight of the office door. He rang Tiger to give him the results of his snooping then settled down behind the box to wait for Iago to reappear.

At six o'clock, Iago and Dilys were at their usual places at the bar of the Glendower Arms. Summers had not yet shown up, but there were a few other patrons drinking there in solitary silence.

'How's the big case going, Mr Price?' asked Lewis Evans, with heavy, but good-humoured sarcasm.

Iago tapped the side of his nose confidentially.

'Fine, fine. Can't give you any details, but my reputation is spreading, eh, Dilys?' He again took the opportunity of patting her thigh and she pulled it away with an impatient jerk.

'Fine?' she echoed cynically. 'All you've done is to follow some feller to a cafe down the docks – and you're going to have the cheek to charge a fiver, plus a bus fare and taxi ride for that! I know what I'd tell you, if I was him!'

Iago made futile shushing noises, and looked furtively around the saloon. His eyes passed over Archie Vaughan, but were none the wiser. Archie sat as near as possible to the pair at the bar and his large ears had picked up useful confirmation of earlier happenings.

Iago turned back to his secretary.

'Don't discuss business in here, Dill. I've told you often enough.'

The blonde sniffed haughtily. 'About as often as you've asked me to go out with you.'

He scowled at her. 'I've stopped asking,' he sulked.

She shrugged indifferently. 'There's a pity! I would have said yes tonight.'

Iago gaped at her. A full-size, slack-jawed gape.

'You would? Tonight?'

Dilys sniffed again. 'May as well. Nothing else to do.' Iago clutched her hand as if she had just saved him from drowning.

'Marvellous! Some good films on, we could have a meal afterwards.'

She stared at him sternly. 'No funny business then, or I'll belt you!'

Iago gabbled assurances of his virtuous intentions, none of which he intended to keep. He drained his glass and slid it across the bar.

'Drink up, love, this needs celebrating! Lewis, let's have some service.'

The brawny landlord came across, his hairy forearms rippled as he pulled a pint for Iago after Dilys' champagne perry.

'Gone soft in the head, Dill?' he enquired solicitously. 'Hot blood Iago Price here will expect your virtue after a film, a fried rice and a small shandy, mind.'

Dilys flapped her heavily blackened eyelids at him.

'I've ate better things than him before breakfast, Lewis love.' Her Cardiff accent sounded stronger than ever, but it was music in Iago's ears.

Archie Vaughan shifted impatiently on his seat at all

this useless small talk. He looked anxiously at his watch. There had been no word from Bute Street since mid-afternoon and Archie was wondering how long he should keep up this shadowing lark.

His mind was promptly made up at that moment.

The door opened and in came Summers. The ferrety man knew him well by sight – he had good cause to, as it was he who had taken the photographs in Betty's bedroom, an uncomfortable operation including three hours' incarceration in a wardrobe.

The bank security man looked around suspiciously. He sat next to Iago and spoke so softly that Archie could not catch a single word. Then Iago produced a piece of paper and slid it across the bar to Summers, who looked at it, then called for a pint.

This was enough for Archie Vaughan. He left his drink unfinished and slipped out, making for the nearby telephone box.

Chapter Three

Bob Ellis jerked his feet off the desk and threw down the library book in disgust.

'Bloody trash! I don't know why I bother to read 'em!' he snorted in the direction of a detective constable, who sat at the next desk painstakingly typing a statement with two fingers, his tongue struck out as an aid to concentration.

'What don't you like about it, Ellis?' came a deep voice from behind.

The detective inspector jumped up and reddened a little.

'Oh, hello, sir. Didn't hear you come in. I was talking about these damn silly crime novels. I'm like a drug addict; I despise them, but I can't give them up!'

A brief mechanical smile flickered across the long saturnine face of the other man, then he promptly lost interest. He walked away towards his own room at the end of the Criminal Investigation Department, then called back over his shoulder, 'Anything doing this evening?'

Ellis shook his head. 'Very quiet, thank God. This fog and drizzle are keeping the villains at home. I'm just waiting for a call from the Crime Squad about that supermarket job in Llandaff.'

The chief superintendent grunted and vanished into his office. Bob Ellis looked at the closed door with mixed curiosity and relief. Meredith had only been back in Cardiff a matter of weeks, but already his nickname had followed him and stuck fast, as fast as his London reputation for ruthless dealing. His dark face, upturned black eyebrows and his Christian name of Nicholas had made ‘Old Nick’ an inevitable tag.

Meredith had left the Swansea Valley over twenty years before to join the Metropolitan Police and had risen to detective superintendent at the Yard. Now he had fulfilled his yearning for Wales by being appointed the new chief of the CID in the Welsh capital, jumping up another rank in the process.

It was early days yet for the rest of the force to make up their minds about Old Nick. Being a new boss was always a disadvantage in any popularity contest, but already his staff were impressed with his know-how, if a little wary of his dour ways and his subtle, if infrequent, humour.

Bob Ellis shrugged and sat down again, wondering whether to attack the pile of papers in his ‘In’ tray while waiting for the call.

The DC tapped painfully away alongside him, but the rest of the long room was deserted. It was half-past seven in the evening and the rest of the Headquarters staff were either out on routine jobs or had vanished homewards through the mist-shrouded park that housed the civic buildings that were the pride of the city.

A phone suddenly shrilled on one of the empty desks, next to the typist.

‘It’ll be the Squad, for me,’ said Ellis.

The constable listened, then shook his head. ‘No, but it’s for you. Dai Rees from “A” Division.’

Ellis went to the phone and listened to the voice at the other end for quite a time.

‘Think there’s anything in it?’ he asked dubiously.

He heard Meredith’s door opening behind him and sensed that the chief was listening.

The ‘A’ Division man talked again, then Ellis said, ‘I’ll come across, though it sounds a load of rubbish to me.’

He put the phone down and turned to find Meredith standing over him, his lanky six-foot one stooping like some old raven. Old Nick wore his winter uniform of long black overcoat, grey scarf and carried a black Anthony Eden hat in his gloved hand. Ellis was strongly reminded of an undertaker he knew, from one of the mining valleys.

'Anything happening?' rasped the chief-superintendent. Ellis thought again that he had the common failing of practical men who reached the top by hard work – they are unable to delegate responsibility, thinking they can do everything better themselves.

Ellis rubbed his ear thoughtfully. 'Odd story, but sounds a lot of bullshine to me, sir.'

He stopped and Meredith waited with an impatient look on his face. The watching constable thought what a difference there was between the cadaveric face of Old Nick and the plump, cheerful Ellis, with his gingery hair and pink, shiny skin. But they both had one thing in common: they were equally devoted to the catching of villains.

Ellis got his tongue into gear again. 'Two chaps have been involved in a hit-and-run, sir. One seriously injured, the other only scratches and shock.'

Meredith's curved eyebrows rose in enquiry. 'Since when have CID been involved in traffic accidents?'

'One of these men is a bank security officer, the other is a private enquiry agent. The first was badly hurt and the other started to holler for the law as soon as he came around from his slight concussion.'

Both the DC and the chief superintendent waited for the punchline.

'The uniformed men asked Dai Rees – he's a detective sergeant, "A" Division, as you probably remember, sir – they asked him to go over to the Infirmary, as this private eye chap alleged that the running-down was deliberate, not an accident. Sounds a right lot of old nonsense to me, but I'd better go over and sort it out.'

Meredith brooded for a second.

'What's wrong with "A" Division doing their own dirty

work?'

Ellis had the answer for this one already. 'The DI is on the sick, sir. Fell down and broke his wrist this morning.'

Old Nick grunted. 'All right, sounds a lot of cobblers to me, especially if there's a Nosy Parker involved. But let me know what happens. The attempted murder of a private eye would be a new one, even for me!'

He loped away towards home and a few minutes later, Ellis followed him out to go to the Royal Infirmary.

At ten thirty that night, subdued voices came from a cubicle in the Accident Ward of the hospital.

Iago Price slumped in the bed, his head swathed with a dramatic, if unnecessary, bandage. There was sticking plaster on his chin, and a few more pieces on his hands. He was shaking a little, but as much from suppressed rage as from shock.

'Not a damned word did they believe, the thick-headed morons!' he snarled with muted passion.

Dilys Thomas sat alongside the bed, patting her elaborate hairdo and trying unsuccessfully to look sympathetic.

'Sorry I couldn't come before, but after you didn't turn up, I happened to meet a boyfriend. We went to the pictures.'

Iago smiled thinly. 'Only time you ever agreed to come out with me, and someone tries to murder me!'

Her usually impassive face wrinkled impatiently. 'Come off it, Iago! You're no big wheel in this city! Who would want to rub you out?'

Her diet of films and television had warped her local accent into a weird dialect. Iago's face darkened again.

'Even you call me a liar! I tell you, this car came right at us, up on the pavement. I was lucky, being on the outside, as I could jump clear. But poor old Summers got bounced against the wall. They don't know if he'll live.'

He nodded his turbaned head in the direction of the main ward, where a nurse sat beside a deeply unconscious Summers.

Dilys shifted on her stool and demurely pulled her miniskirt straight, though as an aid to modesty, it was no more use than a wide belt.

'What did the police say, then?' she asked, just to humour him.

Iago sneered, until he found it hurt his bruised chin. 'Say? They just sat and looked sympathetic and didn't believe a damn word.' His pale eyes looked watery, and for a moment the girl thought he was going to cry.

'Did you tell them all about Summers?' she asked.

'I had to, didn't I? Dropped him in the mire, I suppose, but this has gone a bit further than blackmail now.'

Dilys shifted restlessly. The boyfriend was waiting outside, itching to get down to the serious part of the evening.

'Are they going to do anything about it?' she made herself ask.

Iago tried to snarl this time. 'Said they'd look into it – like hell they will. If Summers was able to talk to them, they'd listen. He's a respectable bank official, but me – I'm just a pain in their collective neck,' he muttered bitterly. 'I'll bet they went outside, put their little pencils back in their notebooks and said "he's just a nutcase" or "suffering from shock, poor chap".'

'He didn't seem to be a nutter, sir – and the doctor said he was hardly shocked at all by the time I saw him. They're letting him go home this morning.'

Bob Ellis stood in front of Meredith's desk, with his notebook open and at the ready.

Old Nick looked up from his chair and rubbed his blue-black chin ruminatively. With his colouring, he could never get a decent shave, he always had a 'five o'clock shadow' by ten in the morning.

'Do you think he's talking sense?'

The detective inspector nodded. 'I think *he* thinks he's telling the truth. Whether he's having delusions after the bump on the head is another matter. The quacks said they'd no reason to think so.'

Meredith brooded again for a moment. 'He gave you this yarn about Summers being blackmailed and going to him for help,' he recapitulated. 'Then Summers came to meet him at the Glendower Arms. What time did they leave, did he say?'

'About a quarter to seven. Price was going to walk with Summers to his car, then go back to the pub.'

'Where had Summers left his car?'

'On a demolished site – that part of the town has more car parks than buildings now. This particular one was further down the side street where Price has his office. He said they were just getting to the gap in the fence where you drive in, when a pair of headlights rushed straight at them, right up on the pavement.'

Old Nick was building his own mental picture of the scene, trying to find faults. It was a technique that often paid off.

'If he says that Summers was badly hurt because he was thrown against the wall, where was the wall?'

Ellis looked in his notebook. 'The Panda patrol said that Summers was crushed against one of the concrete pillars holding up the chain link fencing.'

The chief superintendent nodded his long chin. 'Why is Price so convinced this was deliberate and not just an accidental running-down?'

'They were well onto the pavement – there were no cars or other obstructions in the road to cause this vehicle to swerve. He says it accelerated and came up over the kerb at them.'

'Could have been a drunk,' objected Meredith.

Ellis shrugged. 'Could be, I suppose. A bit early, before seven o'clock.'

'No witnesses at all?'

'Not one. It's a free car park, no attendant at night. We'll put out a call on radio and telly, but it's a faint hope. Everyone seems to get instant blindness at times like this.'

Meredith grunted. 'Is this bank chap in real danger – medically, I mean?'

'Pretty bad. The doctors were thinking of operating this morning, but the indications aren't right. They don't know what might happen to him – he might suddenly wake up or die – or just stay flat out indefinitely.'

Meredith chewed at the loose skin around his fingernails. It was the only sign he ever gave of the pressures bottled up inside him.

'So until he comes round we've only got Price's word for all this yarn?'

'That's about it, sir.'

Old Nick had another meal off his index finger.

'Think it's worth following up? You're the one that saw Price.'

Bob Ellis was cautious. 'I feel we'll have to ask around a bit, even if only to satisfy ourselves that it's all a lot of nonsense.'

'This chap Price. What do we know about him?'

Ellis shrugged. 'No reason to think he's a villain or a crackpot. He's the only son of a well-to-do businessman, retired now. The son was a bit of a disappointment to the old man. The father is a real go-getter shipping tycoon, but Iago has been a wash-out. Not in a bad way, just one of nature's failures.'

Meredith seemed interested. *A go-getter in his own grim way, perhaps deadbeats were a novelty to him*, thought Ellis. Aloud, he said, 'Iago has been in about a dozen jobs so far. He was chucked out of the university for failing his exams – then he started in his father's business and got the push from there.'

'His dad threw him out?' asked Old Nick.

'Well, more or less. He set him up in a little bookseller's business, but that fell flat in about three months. I hear the old man just about washed his hands of the son then. He went selling cars, touting for advertisement space and finally to flogging cheap furniture.'

'Where did this detective business come in then?'

'About a year ago – he started from scratch with the usual divorce and status enquiry stuff. He seems to be existing, if nothing else. Apart from an office girl, his overheads are about nil. His office is over a condemned shop!'

Meredith looked hard at Ellis. 'You seem to know a hell of a lot about him.'

'My brother works in the dad's shipping office. And since Price has started on this private detective lark, I made it my business to know more about him. I keep tabs on all the enquiry agents, though the rest are in a far bigger way of business than Iago. They think he's a big joke.'

Meredith studied Ellis from under his overhanging eyebrows. 'So you don't think he's bent?'

'No, he hasn't got the brains. He's an inoffensive sort of chap, never grown up, really. Everyone feels sorry for him, that's how he gets by, I reckon. Hardly ever goes near the old man, though I expect that his mum slips him the odd cheque now and then. They can afford it, God knows.'

Meredith suddenly seemed to decide that he had spent enough time on Iago Price.

'Well, do what you think necessary. Let me know if anything comes of it.'

He picked up some papers and a pen. Ellis took the hint and went back into the main CID room.

The same detective constable was still laboriously pecking away at his typewriter, though presumably he had been home to sleep.

'Give that a bloody rest, Williams, your tongue is getting frostbite,' ordered Ellis. 'I want you to come down to the Docks with me. You've never been stationed at Bute Street, have you?'

The gangling young detective constable, with a deceptively vacant manner, was thankful for an excuse to leave his typewriter.

'Docks, sir? No, spent my time at Ely and Roath.'

Ellis nodded in satisfaction. 'Good, I want a strange face. You might even get a cup of coffee at the police force's expense if you play your cards right!'

The mystified Williams followed him out to the car park.

Chapter Four

'You're the biggest damned menace I've ever had working with me!'

Tiger Ismail paced the carpet of his upstairs room, looking more than ever like his animal namesake. He padded from wall to wall in suppressed rage, hands gripped behind him so tightly that the knuckles showed white. His smooth, tan face was hard with temper and his eyes had a glitter that made Nikos Kalvos very uneasy.

'I'm sorry, Tiger,' he mumbled for the fourth time, 'I'd had a couple too many. How the hell was I to know that Archie would want me all of a sudden?'

Ismail stopped and wheeled around. For a second, the Greek thought he was going to strike him.

'Nikos, when I send to tell you to duff up a couple of guys, I mean with your bloody fists – not the front end of a Morris Oxford!'

Archie Vaughan sat in a corner, trying to look inconspicuous, but Tiger swung around on him next.

'You did tell Nikos to collect Joe Davies and give them a hammering, didn't you?' he snapped accusingly.

Archie nodded rapidly.

'Just like you said, Tiger. As soon as I saw Summers and that private dick in the pub, I ran out and phoned you. You said ring 'em, so I got Nikos on the blower in the Dollies Club and tells him 'zactly what you said.'

The pock-faced Greek writhed his shoulders at this and turned up his palms in supplication.

'I couldn't find Joe, honest! You said it was a rush job, so I picked up a barrow and thought that a little push with the front fender would do the trick just as well.'

'And what if you'd killed them!' snarled Tiger. His voice stayed low, but lost none of its menace. 'You may still have croaked Summers, according to what I hear. If he dies, Nikos, you're on your own, I don't want to know. Get that, Archie, that goes for you too!'

Nikos and Archie nodded hastily, each offering up a quick prayer that the bank man would stay in the land of the living.

Tiger threw himself angrily into a chair. Even in such a careless movement, he seemed to flow naturally into a supple position, like a practised ballet dancer.

'If Joe had been there, it wouldn't have been cocked up like this. I wanted those two duffed up in some alleyway. And from behind, so they wouldn't recognize anyone. A few black eyes and a belt over the head wouldn't have taken half a minute. Then Joe could have gone today with a nice message to Summers to say he'd had his last chance, and that drip of a private eye would have had the frighteners put on him so that he'd stay clear and keep his mouth shut.'

'Well, they're frightened all right now!' said Kalvos with a touch of bravado.

'You damn fool!' said Tiger. 'The coppers will be crawling all over them. How do you know one of them didn't get a description of the car?'

'It was nicked!' objected Nikos in an injured voice.

'So what? In a case like this, the bobbies will pull out all the stops, especially if Summers snuffs it. They'll find the car, maybe get prints from it. Then you're right up the creek.'

The Greek strong-arm man muttered something about gloves, but Tiger wasn't listening. He uncoiled from the chair and glided over to the bar, where he poured a stiff brandy for himself. He offered nothing to the other two, who were in disgrace.

Heavy feet sounded on the stairs outside and Joe Davies came in. As Tiger's first lieutenant, he was much less cowed by him than the other two. He grinned at their obvious discomfiture and helped himself to a drink. He was no genius, but he knew just how far he could go with Tiger.

Ismail glowered at him. 'What's the whisper from up town?'

The long-haired newcomer shrugged. 'All quiet on the bleedin' Western Front. They let that skinny bloke outta' the Infirmary this morning. Summers is still flaked, so one of the porters told me.'

'Any sign of the coppers taking an interest?'

'They called last night to see this chap Price. Can't see much activity today, though.'

Even Tiger's efficient organization had no means of knowing that Detective Constable Williams was at that very moment sitting downstairs, drinking tea and chomping a thick ham roll amongst the midday workmen that provided most of the custom for the Cairo Restaurant.

There was silence in the lounge as Tiger brought his considerable IQ to bear on the situation.

Perhaps he had been wrong to bring his operations into the city, he thought. It was fouling one's nest to break the previous rules of only playing away from home.

For the past few years, they had been working steady rackets well away from Cardiff, taking care never to leave a trail back to Bute Street, even if it meant abandoning a job. Tiger had never heard the aphorism 'better to run and fight another day' but he carried out its sentiments to the letter.

Hijacking transported goods from heavy lorries had been their favourite pastime for two years. Nikos was the motorman of the team. With Archie, Joe or one of the other members of the gang, he would go to Newport, Bristol or Worcester, steal a van and make for a transport cafe where big trucks were parked. With or without the driver's connivance, they would drive away a lorry-load of cigarettes or valuable mixed goods and transfer the best pickings to the van. After taking the loot to a pre-arranged hideout or a waiting receiver, they would dump the van and filter back to Cardiff by public transport.

As time went on without a single scare from the police, Tiger became more ambitious, but none the less cautious. A few breaking-and-entering jobs were added to their repertoire, with Nikos again useful as a lock-picker and moderately efficient safe-breaker. More recently still, some smuggling was added to the list. Tiger never figured in any operation. He was the planning department and saw to it that no pattern of method ever developed. He had a healthy respect for the police, especially their Criminal Records Office, where details of the 'modus operandi' were meticulously kept. By widening their range of activities, he calculated that there would be less chance of some clever chair-bound policeman lighting on similarities in pattern.

A few months before, by sheer chance, an event occurred which tempted Tiger to play at home in Cardiff. Joe caught his current girlfriend in a compromising position with a strange man. Though Joe was not particularly disturbed – a few black eyes would have squared the matter and 'birds' were two a penny to him – the man caught red-handed was so terrified that he babbled an offer to help them rob a large shop in Cardiff, where he was assistant manager. As a result, the gang cleaned up a satisfactory amount of cash and movable goods with no effort at all.

This set Tiger thinking of a repeat performance.

Perhaps too ambitiously for a first attempt, they set up the blackmail trap for Summers, using the same girl, Betty. Tiger now realized that they had set their sights too high, though it might have come off but for the moronic behaviour of the Greek. Now it was all off, with the added fear of a manslaughter charge waiting for somewhere to roost, if Summers died.

He swilled his drink around in his glass and thought that there were plenty of other less tough nuts to crack. Better to spend a month working up another, than seven years 'over the wall'.

'So what we going to do now?' asked Joe Davies, putting the boss's thoughts into words.

'This one is a write-off,' murmured Tiger, his face expressionless as his temper subsided. 'As long as Nikos doesn't get nobbled for a killing, we'll look around for something else.'

'Goin' to set Betty up for some other sucker?' leered Archie. He was the only one not to have made the grade with the easy-going Betty. Even she couldn't stomach the rat-like little man with the mouthful of rotten teeth. As a result, Archie had to make do with the vicarious thrills like the wardrobe episode.

Tiger Ismail glared at him. 'We've sucked that one dry for the time being. Perhaps we were out of our class there.'

He was a realist, this Tiger. Too many criminals failed because of a built-in God complex, in his estimation. One piddling success and they become megalomaniacs, which made them careless. No, the blackmail angle was out, but there should still be something similar to that shop raid, which had been a profitable pushover.

He threw down the last of his drink and stood up sinuously.

'Joe, take Timmy and Les, as you're the three glamour boys in this outfit. Start picking up some of the girls from the big stores up in town. Don't do anything yet, just get to know them, then when you're well in, pump them for anything useful about the shops, like cash movements, security, anything.'

Timmy and Les were two of Tiger's distant relatives,

young and smooth. Though from his own family, they showed no obvious foreign blood, but had a great reputation for getting around women.

Joseph Stalin Davies smiled happily.

'A pleasure, Tiger – but are we reduced to knocking over shops now?'

The leader frowned. 'I'm not after boxes of nylons or fish forks, Joe. Some nights, especially now before Christmas, these shops carry as much cash as the banks. With the right bit of information, we could pull off a single job that would set us up. You just get talking to these dollies, especially any you can find from the accounts offices.'

He turned back to look at Nikos Kalvos. 'Meanwhile, we'll go back to the lorries, if we can keep the Greek sober!'

'A lot's happened since you last sat there, Iago!'

Lewis Evans' deep voice brimmed over with morbid complacency.

'Job's comforter!' grunted Price. 'You haven't said yet how glad you are to see me alive.'

He sat in his usual place at the bar, but without Dilys this time. She had already been spirited away by one of her numerous boyfriends all of whom were after the same thing as Iago.

'Your head don't look so bad, man,' boomed Lewis cheerfully. He rubbed briskly at a pint glass and stared with interest at Iago's plasters. The enquiry agent gingerly touched the large one on his temple that had replaced the original bandage.

'A nasty graze under here – and on these.' He held up a hand to show the Elastoplast stuck over his knuckles.

'Still, you're lucky not to be where that other chap is!' said the landlord in a sepulchral voice that suggested that Summers was already in the mortuary.

Iago nodded. 'Poor fellow is still in a coma, the Infirmary says.'

Lewis looked around the bar. Apart from the old man with the spaniel, it was empty. Although satisfied that there were no eavesdroppers, he lowered his voice to a conspiratorial whisper. 'Funny thing, Iago – the other night there was a little chap sitting there at the first table. Came in right after you and I felt he was there for a purpose. As soon as Mr Summers came in and put his head together with you, this fellow took off like a dog out of a trap – didn't even finish his drink.'

He shrugged and rubbed away again at the already gleaming glass. 'May be nothing in it, mind, but I never seen him before and this house only attracts regulars, being off the beaten track.'

Iago digested this in silence. He had not noticed the man on the previous evening, but Lewis Evans was an observant chap. Could this fellow be connected with the near-fatal onslaught by that car? Today, as the fright and outrage wore off, Iago began to have doubts and wondered if the whole thing really was an accident, as the police seemed to imply, but the landlord's suspicions about an eavesdropper in the bar brought back his feeling that Summers' troubles were at the root of it. With the decision came a slow anger.

Summers was out of the running, maybe for good. The police would do nothing apart from some polite listening unless some new development forced them to believe Iago's story.

Something must be done, but what? Iago might have been a slow thinker and have a brain a long way from the Einstein class, but he was no moron. Nor was he a hero bent on suicide in the cause of justice. The next motorcar might do more than bruise him. Something must be done, but he had no intention of doing it personally. He opened his overcoat and settled down on his stool with a mental gesture of determination.

'Lewis, got a minute?'

The dark, hairy landlord came across and leant over the bar.

'Lewis, do you know any chaps who aren't fussy what they have to do for a few quid?'

The black brows corrugated. 'What sort of thing? A punch-up?'

Iago shook his head, his straggling hair bobbing on his narrow forehead. 'I want someone to have a damn good snoop around that cafe in Bute Street; whatever is going on, that place is the centre. I want to know who lives there, what goes on there – that sort of thing.'

'That's the police's job,' objected the landlord.

'Police! They think I'm a nutcase. They'll do nothing unless they're prodded into it – and I'd like to do the prodding.'

Lewis Evans pondered over Iago's request, drawing wet circles in the spilt beer on the polished top of the bar. Iago thought that he was being reluctant.

'I can't do it myself – I've been into the Cairo Restaurant already – they know me now,' he wheedled.

Lewis still doodled wetly on his counter. 'I know plenty of young tearaways who'd skin their mothers for half a quid. But this calls for brains, not muscle power.'

He looked up suddenly. 'Drop it, Iago, there's a good lad. You'll only get hurt again and what else can you expect to get out of it. Summers is hardly likely to be paying anybody from now on, except an undertaker.'

Iago's face became stubborn.

'I'm damned if anyone is going to run me over and get away with it,' he said obstinately. 'God knows, I'm far from being flush, but I can still afford a few pounds to try to get some satisfaction, even if it's only seeing the police stir off their backsides.'

Lewis pushed himself away from the bar and rubbed

his hands slowly.

'There is a chap, a fellow called Terry Rourke. Real villain, done time, but he's been going straight lately. He's one of these likeable yobs, you know? Mad Irishman, though he's hardly ever left Cardiff, except to go to the nick. Pinch the shirt off your back, but buy you a pint while he's doing it!'

'How old is he?'

'About twenty-three, twenty-four. Working in the fruit market now, heaving spuds and cabbages about. Comes in here most nights, later on when the girls are in.'

'Think he'd be any good at the kind of thing I want? asked Iago dubiously.

'Just the lad! He might even do it for nothing, for the hell of it. But certainly, if you slip him a few quid for beer and birds, he'd be there like a shot. Anything to get him away from real work!'

'When could I see him?'

'I'll have a word tonight, then he can come over the office tomorrow. Mind, you want to keep Dilys locked away or he'll have her across the desk inside five minutes!'

This set off a different train of thought in Iago's mind and he sat sulking over his drink until it was time for him to slink home to his lonely flat in Cathedral Road.

Dilys was wetting the instant coffee for 'elevenses' when the office door opened. Before she could put down the battered electric kettle, an arm had slipped around her waist.

'Hi, darling, what you doin' tonight?'

A total stranger grinned impudently at her from a range of six inches. She brought her hand back for an Olympic standard slap, then found that she didn't want to do it. Almost reluctantly, she rotated out of his grasp and moved around the desk.

‘Didn’t hear you knock, sonny,’ she said with unconvincing coldness.

Terry Rourke grinned back roguishly. He was a smaller version of Joe Stalin Davies, wavy black hair, sideboards and tight trousers, but he was brighter-eyed and altogether more agile than Tiger’s henchman. The general effect was almost bird-like, a virile bantam cockerel!

‘Hello, me love! Is the gaffer in?’

There was a genuine Irish undertone to his local accent. His parents had come from Cork to have their twelve children in Cardiff.

Dilys sniffed haughtily, but her eyes were actively sizing him up. ‘Proper yob, but fun with it,’ was her mental verdict. Aloud, she tried to be the supercilious private secretary.

‘Have you got an appointment with Mr Price?’ *Cut him down to size*, she thought.

Rourke let his eyes travel down her body, undressing her as they went.

‘Come off it, pet!’ he pleaded, still looking at her legs. ‘I knocked down better dumps than this when I was on the demolition.’

The inner door suddenly opened. The partition was about as soundproof as wet newspaper and Iago had heard all the crosstalk.

‘Are you Terry Rourke?’

‘S’right, guvnor. Lloyd George sent me over.’

For some obscure reason, Rourke always referred to the landlord by this name, possibly because it was the only well-known Welshman of whom he had ever heard.

Iago beckoned him into the office. With a last lascivious survey of Dilys, which warmed her up all over, the young reprobate went in and took the solitary chair opposite Iago.

The enquiry agent slapped a pound note on the desk in front of Rourke.

'That's for nothing and for keeping your mouth shut. Take it when you leave if we don't fix anything between us.'

He had few pounds to throw away like this, but a rare flash of intuition told him that this kind of approach might pay dividends with an impressionable character like Rourke.

The younger man whipped it up joyfully. 'Spit it out, squire! This sort of talk I understand!'

'Did Lewis Evans tell you what it was all about?'

Terry shook his head and Iago gave him an outline of the story from the beginning.

'So naturally I want to find out what goes on in this crummy eating house,' he wound up finally.

Terry sat strangely subdued. 'This all on the level?' was all he asked.

Iago was nettled. No one seemed keen to believe a word he said. 'What do you think I'm wearing this for – a decoration?' he snapped, touching the plaster on his forehead.

'OK, OK, I was only asking,' muttered the Irish boy. 'For, if you're talking on the level, it means playing with some very rough boys.'

Iago stared at him. 'You know who they are?'

Terry pulled out a filthy comb and began to rake back the long hair off his temples.

'Yeah – and how! The Cairo joint is the pad of Tiger Ismail and his boys. The guy you followed could only be Joe Davies, Tiger's main sidekick.'

He stopped and looked puzzled. 'This don't seem like Ismail's usual line of country. Not blackmail, or knocking over banks. Unless he's getting big ideas all of a sudden.'

Iago was excited at this rapid widening of his knowledge without even leaving the office. He pressed Terry for more details.

'Tiger? Sure, everybody knows him down the Bay,'

replied Rourke. 'He's got a bit of wog in him, though his brothers don't look like him. Bloody great family they are, dozens of cousins and uncles and aunts. They got a finger in half the rackets that go on down the docks. Cleverer than most, too.'

'How do you mean, clever?' asked Iago.

'They don't get nicked so often. Tiger never gets nicked at all. Only the tiddlers on the edge of the gang ever get knocked off by the fuzz. A few of the girls are on the game and some of the kids spend most of their time on probation for lifting stuff from shops. But the big boys keep their noses clean.'

Iago didn't see why such an obvious set of crooks like this couldn't be capable of a bank robbery, and said so.

Terry looked uneasily about him. He dropped his voice a little.

'Knocking off lorries full of fags and cracking empty houses is more their line of country – that and exporting pinched motors to the Midlands. Though for Christ's sake don't pass that on, will you? I don't want Joe Davies to come and alter the shape of me head!'

Iago was unconvinced.

'Well, I know for sure they're getting up to bigger rackets than that. And I wanted you to get some information that might nail them. They tried to alter the shape of my head, too!' He touched his temple gingerly to make his point clearer.

Terry nibbled a fingernail uneasily. 'What do you want me to do? I don't fancy getting across that lot, mind,' he muttered.

Iago started to scratch his head until he found that it hurt.

'You've told me a bit of what I wanted to know already. But what about this running-down the other night? Who would be most likely to have done that?'

Terry Rourke shrugged.

'I don't know all the angles, mister. I've always kept well clear of the Tiger mob. With all that family, it's mainly a closed shop, but there are a few outsiders like Joe Davies and Archie Vaughan.'

'What about this cafe? Is that just a front?'

'Naw, it's full of folks at dinner time or late at night. Some of the girls use it and there used to be a fair trade in betting slips before they made it legal. But it's a proper "caff" all right.'

'Who runs it, then?'

'Florrie, Tiger's aunt. Don't think it belongs to her, but who knows. I tell you, I've always kept clear.'

Iago waited a moment, then took the plunge. 'Look, if I made it worth your while, could you hang around there and see what you can pick up?'

Rourke looked shocked. 'Grass on 'em? I wouldn't do that, it's against me principles! Besides, they'd have my guts for garters if I was rumbled.'

Iago Price leaned over the desk.

'Look, it wouldn't be grassing; it would be to me, not the police. They tried to flatten me the other night, don't you think I've got a right to a comeback?'

This appealed to Rourke's sense of fair play. His good spirits were returning after the first uneasiness of hearing that Tiger was involved. He would have done well in the days of the highwaymen and pirates.

'I'm still on licence after the last stretch, but this ain't illegal, is it? I'll see what I can do. But what's in it for me?'

After some haggling, Iago agreed to pay him twenty pounds for a week's work, providing he came up with some useful information. The detective saw himself writing another begging letter to his mother, who was on an extended winter holiday in the Tyrol, but he consoled himself with the thought that a single week should prove if the whole idea was a flop or not.

With a promise to keep in touch via the phone and the pub, Terry left the office. On the way out, he pinned Dilys to the partition and gave her a ravishing kiss.

'See you in the boozer tonight, love,' he promised. With a lecherous wink, he was gone.

Iago stood morosely in his doorway watching the girl coming back to earth. 'He got further with you in ten minutes than I have in ten months!' he said sourly.

'Cheeky swine!' breathed Dilys, but there was a faraway look in her eyes as she ran her tongue around her lips. Iago went back inside and slammed the door so hard that a snowstorm of loose plaster fluttered gently down.

Chapter Five

A black Austin Westminster pulled up outside a grimy red-brick building which stood in lonely isolation amongst a sea of tumbled rubble.

Built in the days when the sun never set on the British Empire, the Bute Street police station was nearing the end of its life. Only the fact that its new glass-and-chrome replacement was not yet ready, reprieved it from the same fate as the surrounding landscape.

Nicholas Meredith and Bob Ellis left the car and pushed through the battered green doors into the dismal interior.

'Not worth painting, hardly worth even cleaning, by the look of it,' murmured Old Nick, staring around the moribund building with distaste.

Ellis had more affection for the old place. He had spent five years as a uniformed constable working out of this Docks Station.

'Wonder how many drunks, whores and thieves have come through those doors,' he mused. 'Must be literally bloody millions!' Certainly, this must surely have been one of the busiest stations in Britain half a century earlier.

But their business was with the present, not the past.

Meredith led the way into the absent detective inspector's room. He was still on the sick, swearing at a new plaster cast on his broken arm.

The detective sergeant from the division, David Rees, was waiting for them in the room and the diffident, skinny DC Williams was hovering nervously in the background.

They talked for a few minutes about various cases and

about the administrative problems raised by the sudden lack of a divisional DI. Then Ellis brought up the relatively trivial matter of Iago Price and his allegations about the Cairo Restaurant.

'You spent a couple of hours sniffing round there yesterday, Williams,' he said almost accusingly. 'Did you get any joy?'

The constable from Headquarters jerked nervously into life. For some reason, Meredith overawed him to the point of speechlessness. He managed to find his tongue this time.

'Couldn't get much, sir. I sat in the cafe for as long as I could without looking like a sore thumb. Had my lunch there, though they'll never make a fortune with their cooking. But I suppose it's as good as any other dive like that.'

Old Nick looked at him impatiently. There seemed to be a mutual bond of irritation between them. 'Damn their cooking, Williams. Who did you see there?'

The DC became even more twitchy and looked appealingly at the Docks sergeant.

'I saw quite a few chaps going in and out. From what Sergeant Rees said later, they must have been the owners, Ismail and the man Davies that Mr Price said he saw in the pub in Queen Street.'

Meredith swung his long face around to the local detective sergeant. 'You know this manor well, I'm sure.

Who uses this cafe? Is it a front? Anything known about it?'

'Anything known' means more to a policeman than the everyday usage of the phrase. Rees, a wiry North Walian, shook his head.

'No convictions, but a lot suspected. Funny set-up, really. Right out of the old days, a cross between Freemasonry and the Mafia.'

Old Nick scowled. 'What the hell d'you mean?' He

liked straight answers, not the parables that this lot seemed to indulge in.

The sergeant explained about the Ismail family gang. Meredith listened, his dark face scowling. 'You mean they're all upright, honest citizens?' he barked at the end. The DS smiled wryly and pulled his ear.

'I've got no evidence to prove otherwise, sir, but it smells! There are about five blokes loafing about that place, never do a stroke of work. They vanish for days at a time, then come back. But they never put a foot wrong. Sometimes we get 'em for drunk and disorderly, but what the hell!'

Williams plucked up courage and spoke again.

'The cafe seems genuine enough, sir. It was nearly full at lunchtime yesterday. An Arab bloke – an old guy – and a fat woman run it.'

Meredith walked up and down in the small room, a difficult exercise as it was half full of furniture and large men.

'You must have your snouts, same as the rest of us. What do they say?'

Dai Rees shrugged. 'Not much "grassing" down here, sir. The population is as honest as anywhere else these days – more so than many places. But even the good 'uns stick together like glue. It's more like a village than part of a city, this. Once you come under that bridge from town, it's a separate little world. They keep their lips buttoned on principle.'

Old Nick made a face suggesting that this was all sanctimonious claptrap. 'You must have an ear to the ground somewhere!'

The sergeant shuffled his feet.

'Well, it's more intuition than information, but I think they work the trucks away from home. We had a whisper a couple of years ago and went and worked their place over on grounds of receiving. We used a toothcomb on the cafe and didn't find even the dust of any loot. Then Ismail sicked a lawyer on to us and even started an action for illegal entry. Didn't get anywhere, but we had to be careful after that.'

Bob Ellis nodded. 'I remember that. We were told we wouldn't get any more warrants without cast-iron evidence. There hasn't been a twitch out of them since then; all laying low as far as Cardiff crimes goes.'

'Any of them with a record?' asked Meredith.

'Only Joe Davies, not counting approved schools and that. Joe did a stretch for robbery with violence, but a fair time back now.'

The chief superintendent eased across to the door. 'So all this guff from our tame private detective is a lot of eyewash?'

Dai Rees twitched his shoulders. 'Nothing to say one way or the other. I wouldn't put any sort of thieving past Tiger Ismail and his mob, but attempted murder isn't his line.'

'Keep an eye on it!' ordered Meredith as he walked out.

Terry Rourke sauntered past the front of the Cairo Restaurant, but made no move to go inside.

He was a wily lad and knew that sitting inside drinking a cup of tea would give him as much insight into the Tiger mob as sitting on the Pier Head staring out to sea.

He walked on slowly as far as the traffic lights at the lower end of Bute Street. Leaning against a shop window, he lit a cigarette and waited for inspiration.

None came, so he made his way back along the pavement towards the cafe. Thirty yards short of it, he saw a narrow alleyway leading to his left. He sidled into it and came out in a wider back lane. Turning right, he found that he was now almost behind Tiger's premises.

Luck started to roll for him at that moment, though if he could have looked further ahead, he would have put as much distance as possible between himself and that lane.

A large red lorry was standing just in front of him, almost blocking the full width of the lane. A rough stone wall, pierced with dilapidated doors, ran along the back of the Bute Street buildings and where the lorry was waiting, a pair of double gates stood open.

A burly, red-faced man in a boiler suit was handing down cardboard cartons from the truck to a tiny old man with a gnarled brown face and a great hooked nose. He was staggering under the impact of massed baked beans as they dropped from the hands of the lorry driver high above him.

Just as Terry began squeezing past the vehicle, there was a frightened squeal as the old man fumbled his catch and dropped a box heavily against the rear mudguard. With a ripping noise, the bottom tore out of the carton and a shower of tins sprayed out, some of them falling on the feet of the old Arab, who began wailing even louder.

The lorry driver began swearing as the tins started to roll under the truck and into the gutter of the cobbled lane.

Seizing the golden opportunity, Terry grabbed the broken box, turned it upside down and quickly collected the tins.

'You go and have a sit down, mate,' he shouted cheerfully at the almost tearful grandfather, who was actually a great-uncle of Tiger's.

'Useless old bugger!' growled the man on the lorry.

'Gimme the rest, mate – you've crippled grandpa for the rest of the day.' Terry slid the broken case inside the gates and held up his arms for another.

Baked beans, flour, rice and all sorts of dry groceries came down until a pile had grown inside the backyard of the Cairo Restaurant.

'Gawd, are they stocking up for a famine?' asked Terry. Work was a sort of allergy to him and he would spend more time and effort in dodging it than in doing an actual job. Only the hope of fiddling an entry to the cafe pushed him into this sudden spurt of activity.

'That's the lot, son. Sign here.' The driver handed down a pink form and a pencil.

'Nothing to do with me, squire, I was just passing. I'll take it and find Abdul, the terrible Turk.'

He was halfway to the back door when it opened and out waddled Florrie, with her usual frizzy hair and carpet slippers.

'All present and correct, missus – here's the chit.'

He handed the invoice over and the woman trundled past him to speak to the lorry driver. On the way back she stopped.

'Ta, son – Uncle Ahmed is getting past it.'

'Want a hand to get 'em inside, missus?' said Terry quickly, afraid that his seam of luck was about to run out.

She stared at him a moment. 'Got nothing else to do?'

The Irish boy grinned. 'I've outstayed me welcome at the Labour Exchange – and I'm too broke to sit in the pub.'

He grabbed the nearest box. 'Where to, mum?'

Florrie jerked a thumb at the rear of the seedy building and he stumbled inside with the box. It was the kitchen entrance and smelled of damp and stale frying. Yet another man with a faint touch of the East was toiling over a grubby sink and a fat man with red hair was sloshing something around in a plastic bowl at a table.

They hardly gave him a glance as he took the box through to a dark storeroom that the woman pointed out to him. He stacked all the rest in there and when he finally came out, Florrie was talking earnestly to the old man.

When Rourke approached, she turned to him. 'Want a temporary job, son? You can pitch in here if you like. One of our lads has gone away for a few weeks.'

'Without the option, eh?' grinned Terry cheekily.

Florrie started to look annoyed, then her sallow face

cracked into a smile. 'You catch on quick. What about it? Odd jobs and kitchen work. Ten quid a week and free grub.'

Terry hesitated long enough to make a convincing show of surprise and uncertainty, then agreed before the manageress could change her mind.

'I'm not a bleeding cook, mind, Ma,' he warned.

She cackled at him. 'Slicing chips and opening tins is the nearest you'll get to cooking, lad. When can you start?'

'No time like the present. I'll begin with some of that grub you promised.'

She grinned again and waddled inside.

After his pie and mash, he was put to washing up after the busy lunchtime rush. When things quietened down in the afternoon, he chatted in pidgin English with Uncle Ahmed, who was one of the few members of the family who had not been born in Cardiff.

He hung about all day, but nothing of importance happened. The only thing that was remotely useful was the appearance at teatime of three men, who came down from the upper floors and immediately left in a waiting car. Terry recognized the lithe figure of Tiger Ismail and the more flamboyant Joe Davies. The other one was unknown to him, but a casual question to the old man gave him the information that this was Nikos the Greek who often drove Tiger's Ford.

Terry stared after the men with some interest. He had not seen the owner of the restaurant for some time; Tiger had become a minor legend amongst the youth of Bute town. These last few years he had lived a secluded life, which added to his air of mystery. Most of the day was spent in his upstairs flat or away from Cardiff altogether, either 'casing' jobs or arranging the disposal of stolen goods. In the evenings and far into the nights he was a familiar figure in the clubs and casinos that had mushroomed in the lower part of the city centre, but there the kids and youths of Dockland were hardly likely to be fellow patrons.

The Irish lad worked the rest of the day out, then went home to the council flat in Riverside, where he lived with his widowed mother and three of the remaining family. His father had drunk himself to death some years earlier and Terry and the National Assistance Board now supported the family.

Next day, the pattern was repeated and by teatime he was itching for some development that would bring the end of this awful work within sight. He had phoned Iago Price that morning to tell him that he was now an employee of Tiger's and that the first day had drawn a blank.

By the early evening, he knew that if he could not think of something to produce a dramatic result by that night, he was going to jack in the whole business.

He watched carefully to see who was going up and down the stairs, but only Tiger and Joe Davies used it that day, apart from some minor members of the family who apparently lived up on the first floor. Terry managed to get as far as this on one occasion and found a warren of small rooms, each with several beds housing part of the Ismail tribe and some offshoots. There was another staircase leading up to the second floor where Tiger lived, but he could find no legitimate excuse to penetrate that far into the enemy camp.

In the hope that the late evening might see more action, he arranged with Florrie to go off at teatime and come back later, as there was a spurt in business when the pubs shut and some drinkers felt the urge for solid food.

About ten o'clock, the three men he had seen the previous day came down the stairs, this time with a weasel-faced man in a cloth cap. Terry had seen him about the district, but did not know his name. They all vanished in the big Ford and left Terry to cast longing glances at the now-deserted stairway.

Waiting for a slack moment, he watched until Uncle Ahmed was in the kitchen. Florrie had gone to a Bingo session, so he slid rapidly up the first flight of stairs. At the top he listened intently, heard nothing and went quickly up the next flight to the upper floor.

He had some experience as a housebreaker, and now it came in handy. The top floor had the feel of being completely deserted and he quickly took bearings on the top landing. There were two doors at right angles, then a long passage leading to the back of the house.

He tried the door of the front room and found it locked. The shrunken frame of the old building left a quarter-inch gap around the door and within a few seconds he was inside, having slid the tongue of the lock back with a piece of stiff plastic, actually a bank credit card stolen months before.

He was afraid to turn on the light, but a street lamp just outside gave plenty of illumination. With the practised hand of the thief, he rapidly went through the room, not knowing what he was looking for, but hoping to find something incriminating.

The few drawers and cupboards had nothing of interest. A writing desk against the wall delayed' him for a moment until he wriggled the simple lock open with a piece of wire from his pocket. The desk was packed with apparently legitimate bills dealing with the restaurant though one bundle, when studied briefly at the window, seemed to be cryptic lists of figures. He risked taking one sheet from the back of the wad, then returned the whole lot to the desk and locked up again. In the corner, covered by a curtain, was an old-fashioned safe, with a brass handle and embossed coat-of-arms. Ancient though it seemed, it was too tough a nut for him to crack, as he was no ‘peterman’.

With a final frustrated glance around the room, he let himself out and clicked the lock shut behind him.

He listened at the head of the stairs but all was quiet.

The next door was open and he slid inside. The windows were covered by heavy curtains and he risked switching on the light.

It was Tiger's bedroom, furnished in expensive modern taste, with a large double bed and fitted wardrobes in gold and white. There was a mirrored dressing table groaning under a profusion of male toilet preparations. On the walls were several large nude photographs, of a frankness that suggested a Scandinavian origin.

It seemed an unlikely room for incriminating evidence, but Terry thought he had better go through the wardrobes and drawers. His hand was on the nearest knob when he heard voices.

In a flash, he was across the room and had knocked up the light switch. There was nothing more he could do but press himself to the wall behind the door and hope for the best.

The voices grew louder as the men came up the stairs. Feet tramped past and then a key rattled in the lock of the front room. Seconds later it slammed shut and he breathed more freely.

Moving over to the partition wall, Terry pressed his ear to the wallpaper. He could hear the muffled sound of voices and the clink of bottles, but no more. Realizing that this was the only chance he was likely to get of hearing something useful, he eased open the door and slipped on to the landing. The voices were louder now, but still unintelligible.

Risking everything, the Irish boy put his ear to the panels of the front room door, eavesdropping at the ill-fitting frame.

Now he could pick up odd snatches of conversation, but only intermittently. People seemed to be walking to and fro, glasses and bottles were still clinking.

As someone walked past, he caught a few clear words:

'… down the Ross motorway on Friday …' Then it faded and a different voice said, 'Any joy with those birds from the shop, Joe? …'

For a moment the footsteps receded and Rourke could pick out nothing at all. Things suddenly got worse as the radio began blaring pop music. He swore at it silently and almost stopped breathing in an effort to pick out a few words of sense.

A moment later someone passed quite near the door – he could feel the floorboards moving.

'… that job should bring us in quite a bit, Tiger.'

The words came so loudly that he was momentarily panic-stricken in case the owner was coming out of the door. It was the voice of Joe Davies, the only one he knew.

Again the voices faded back, but another phrase was just audible.'… gaffer's chips on Sunday night.'

For a full minute after this he could hear nothing. Then a voice almost in his ear said, 'I'll get some more from the bathroom.' A glass chinked and even as Terry dived for the stairs, the door handle started to turn. He was at the foot of the upper flight before the occupant had come out and the solid wall which replaced banisters sheltered him from view. He took a few seconds off to steady his nerves, then went more slowly down to the cafe.

Two customers were waiting to be served and Uncle Ahmed was shuffling along towards them.

'Sorry I was so long, dad. Must have been that shepherd's pie,' he said with a flippancy he didn't feel.

The old Arab said nothing and Terry waited impatiently for the time when he could leave the restaurant, this time for good.

At eleven thirty Florrie came back and said he could go, and he hurried out into the damp, misty December night.

He wanted to justify his fees to Iago Price and lost no time in letting him know his meagre news.

There was a phone box on a corner of West Bute Street, a branch of the main road, just above the Cairo Restaurant. Once inside, he thumbed through a grubby wallet and found Iago's number written on the back of a racing slip. He dialled in the dim light of the overhead bulb and after a long time, the sleepy voice of the private eye came over the line.

He told Iago all that had happened, embroidering it as much as he could to make it sound more important.

'What's all this about "gaffer's chips", for God's sake?' asked Iago petulantly.

'I dunno, Mr Price, but that's exactly what it sounded like.' He spelt out his interpretation for the detective's benefit. 'Gaffer's chips on Sunday. Sounded like Tiger's voice to me.'

After some heavy breathing and thinking, Iago spoke again.

'What are you going to do now?'

Terry Rourke shrugged at himself in the phone box mirror.

'Can't see me getting a better break than I did tonight. I've searched his rooms and listened at his keyhole. Short of "bugging" the place, can't see what else can be done.'

Iago grunted. 'I'll see you right with the money,' he said rashly. 'Better carry on for a day or two. Have a good snoop around the docks to see if you can pick up any tales about Tiger. Try the pubs, that should suit you,' he added unkindly and rang off.

Mention of money brought a satisfied smirk to Terry's face as he pushed his way out of the box.

The smile was short-lived.

He stepped straight into the centre of a silent and very unsmiling group of men – Joe Davies, Nikos the Greek, Archie Vaughan and Uncle Ahmed.

Joseph Stalin grabbed his elbow in a grip like a monkey wrench.

‘And jus’ what was you doin’ upstairs tonight, chum?’ he growled menacingly.

Chapter Six

Cardiff's West Dock was a long, narrow basin, half a mile in length, separated from Bute Street by a high stone wall, a railway and a row of warehouses.

'Was', because after over a hundred years of use, it was nearing the end of its life.

Hundreds of thousands of ships and millions of tons of Welsh coal had passed through its narrow lock gates, but now this was almost a memory. For several years, lorry loads of rubble and ash had laboriously forced the reluctant water out, and on the second day after Iago's late night phone call, only a few yards of grey stone wall and a large pool of dirty water remained.

Two small urchins, mitching from school, had dodged the site watchman and were playing with a tattered mongrel on the steep slope that led down to the edge of the remaining water.

Oblivious of the dangers of an avalanche, the ginger boy skidded down the ramp, yelling and waving his arms. The other one, a gleaming-eyed coloured lad, pointed a piece of wood at him and made machine-gun noises.

'Gotcha! Yer dead!' he screamed, and obediently Ginger fell carefully to the ground and slid the last few feet until his scuffed toecaps were actually touching the water.

The dog slithered down after him, barking rapturously – then suddenly stopped. It began snuffling energetically, then sneezed as the dusty ash went up its nostrils. Not to be put off, it scratched at the water's edge and seized something in its mouth.

A second later, it was bounding up to the dockside, where it dropped its find for a more leisurely inspection.

The two little boys, Commandos forgotten in the new diversion of dog-chasing, scrambled after it. Ginger grabbed it by the tail and the half-caste snatched the dog's prize.

Before they had a chance to look at it, a gruff shout came from behind them. The site foreman had returned from his morning brew-up. He marched across wagging an angry finger in the direction of the entrance gate.

'How many times have I told you kids ...' But the nippers turned tail and fled, the dog barking after them.

The coloured boy flung down something as he went and the foreman bent to pick it up. He scowled down at the pinkish-brown object, then his eyes widened.

Jerking his head up, he stared after the retreating urchins.

'Hey, you ... come here!' and his feet began pounding the rubble as he raced after them.

Two hours later, a uniformed constable stood at the rough gate through the wire boundary fence of the tipping area.

A collection of figures moved slowly over the desolate surface of the filled-in dock. From that distance, they looked like bluebottles crawling on a heap of offal, and a distant view was all the non-privileged were allowed.

A crowd had gathered from nowhere – housewives, workmen, pensioners and a scattering of frustrated newspapermen. A couple of press photographers aimed long-focus lenses to get the usual sterile pictures of bored policemen turning over stones with their boots or of senior plainclothes men standing in earnest groups, discussing last week's football. The real action was down by the water's edge, out of sight of the nosy parkers.

Here Nicholas Meredith, Bob Ellis and Dai Rees, the local sergeant, stood precariously on the ashes and questioned the site foreman. He was a burly, taciturn individual, but a good witness. He thought before he spoke and if he didn't know something, he said so.

'The dog had this thing, then one of the kids – the darkie – took it off him. I grabbed it, thinking it might be something they were trying to pinch, but it was this bone, with teeth in it. By the time I'd sort of realized it, they'd hopped it. I caught up with them just outside the gate. The ginger lad said the dog had found it just here at the water's edge. I made him come back and show me.'

The workman pointed to the centre of the ramp leading into the black water. Two men stood there, inspecting the debris. They were from the Cardiff Home Office Forensic Science Laboratory; one was a scientific officer, the other a detective inspector.

Meredith looked back at the foreman and peered at him sharply from under his beetling brows. He wore his usual 'civvy' uniform and looked more like an undertaker than ever.

'What about all this stuff that's been dumped? If this bone was on the surface, any idea when it was put there?'

The foreman frowned in turn. 'You mean, if it came in the ashes – not just chucked on top?'

Old Nick grunted, 'That's right ... must it have come today?'

The workman hesitated. 'Hell of a job to say, sir. See, we're dumping all along the face of the ramp, to keep the line even. So each truckload goes in a different place ... although the dock is narrow, that means over a hundred yards width.'

Ellis, pink-faced and fresh, cut in here.

'So the load that had this jawbone could have been dumped today, or yesterday – or even before that?'

The workman shook his head. 'Not before yesterday. We tip stuff fast enough to cover the whole face at least once a day, so it couldn't have been on the surface if it had been there very long.' He hesitated again. 'Except …'

'Except what?' snapped Meredith.

The man waved across at the shape of a bulldozer half hidden beneath a tarpaulin.

'Every day, we level off the edge of the tip with that. It mostly pushes new stuff over, but it scrapes a bit of the old as well. So it's possible that hardcore that was put down days ago might get dug up again and rolled over the edge.'

Ellis groaned. 'When did you last use the blade?'

'Last night; we usually tidy up after the day's tipping. It hasn't been used today yet.'

'Nor will it!' added Meredith dourly. 'Not until we've done all we have to here.'

'What about them?' asked the foreman, pointing to three loaded lorries waiting outside the fence.

'Anywhere else you can dump them?' asked Ellis.

'There's a hollow up the other end that would take a bit.'

Old Nick shook his head.

'No, you don't,' he snapped. 'The rest of the bones might still be coming. If we can identify the truck and find where it came from, we might get a lead.'

The foreman was quick to grasp the idea.

'If you square it with my boss, I could get the drivers to tip each load into a separate heap, then someone could keep a record of which truck it came from.'

Meredith beckoned to a uniformed inspector hovering in the background. The business end of a personal radio stuck out from beneath his collar.

'Inspector, call Control Room and ask them if the site contractor has been contacted yet. We want him here, fast!'

He turned back to the foreman. 'Anything else you can tell us.? What about all this stuff' – he swept a hand around the tip – 'Where does it all come from?'

'All sorts of places, sir. We've had a lot of hardcore from the Tiger Bay demolitions, but lately we've been getting boiler ash as well. Comes from factories and big buildings in the neighbourhood.'

He knew no more details and eventually went off with a constable to make a formal statement at the police station. The detectives moved gingerly down the slope to the water's edge.

'Any sign of any more?' Old Nick asked the men from the lab.

The scientist, Roger made a face expressing disgust. 'A few thousand tons of rubble and we're not even sure to a few yards where it was found.'

He was a stocky man with a strong resemblance to Harold Wilson, a gimmick he deliberately cultivated with a pipe and elephant-hide mackintosh. He held the original find in a plastic bag, treasuring it with a reverence more suited to the Holy Grail.

'Think it's been there long?' persisted Meredith.

'No – and it's been burnt. It's brittle and porous. It's not been rained on, so that means it's only been here since last evening at the latest, unless it was buried too deep for the weather to get at it.' He looked up at the leaden sky.

'How do you know it hasn't been wetted and then dried again?' objected Bob Ellis. He had a healthy distrust of scientists.

'Dry! In this weather!' The laboratory man looked scornful. Though not raining, the air was damp and heavy. 'Anyway, there's burnt tissue between the teeth, all crisp and crackly. If it had got wet, it would have collapsed into a slime.'

'Is the pathologist coming?' muttered Meredith.

Ellis looked at his watch. 'Should be here soon. Had an inquest to finish.'

Meredith looked down his nose. 'Better tell the coroner's officer. I don't know what the Cardiff one is like, but some are very much on their dignity and get offended if they're not let in on the act.'

He was interrupted by a triumphant bellow from DI Peter Wade, the laboratory liaison officer. Bending double like a seashell collector on a beach, he had been studying the rubble carefully, occasionally turning a piece over with his fingers. He stood upright holding a brown splinter on his palm.

'More burnt bone! God knows what part of the body, perhaps the doctor will recognize it.'

He bent down again and the rest shuffled nearer.

'Just here, almost in the water,' added Wade.

Within ten minutes, some twenty slivers of brittle bone had been recovered and placed reverently into plastic bags. In a temporary lull in the hunt, Wade looked across at Meredith.

'I think we'll leave this until we can do it properly, otherwise our big feet are going to crush everything.'

Old Nick nodded. He was the boss, but the laboratory angle was Wade's pigeon and his suggestions were to be heeded.

'What do you want us to do?'

'Peg off this area and start looking intensively in square yard plots … move all the big lumps and sieve the small stuff. It all seems to be in this small zone, so it shouldn't be too bad.'

All twenty finds had been in a triangle no more than ten feet across.

'Here's the pathologist, Mr Meredith,' called an officer standing on the top of the slope.

A large, fat Billy Bunter type came slithering down the tip, puffing with exertion.

'Just in time, Doc,' greeted Ellis, who knew him well from many a previous case in the city.

Meredith had never had any dealings with him before and Ellis did the introductions. 'Dr Prosser, from the Medical School, sir. Always clears things up for us, does the doctor.'

Prosser wheezed his greetings and nodded at Peter Wade, a companion on many a previous murder scene.

'What you got for me today, Pete?' he gasped, mopping his round, red face with a handkerchief.

The man from the Home Office handed over the first bag. 'Careful, it's a bit brittle.'

Huw Prosser fumbled in his waistcoat for a pair of steel-rimmed pince-nez, almost falling in the dock as he did so. Screwing them onto his prominent nose, he peered through the polythene, turning the bag this way and that.

Finally he handed it back. 'Ho-ho! Got any more of him?'

Meredith jumped on the words like a terrier on a rat.

'Him? You really mean that?'

The fat pathologist seemed taken aback.

'Well, just a preliminary guess, that's all. Very strong ridges where the jaw muscles were fixed. And a prominent point of the jaw, where it juts out. But don't take that as gospel, at this stage.'

He peered again through his pince-nez at the other bags that the liaison inspector from the laboratory handed to him. 'Fragments and splinters – not a lot of help there, at the moment.'

The inspector pointed to the ashes below them. 'There'll be a lot more when we get a team on this lot,' he said, in satisfaction.

Meredith started to toil up the slope. 'I suggest we get back to ground level. Do less damage to any stuff still here.'

The doctor was blue in the face when they got him up, but as soon as he was able to talk, Old Nick tackled him again. 'First thing, Dr Prosser, this must be a death, I take it? Not just some hospital refuse?'

He remembered bitterly two days wasted in London on a futile murder hunt, only to discover that a dismembered leg on a council tip had been amputated in an operating theatre.

Prosser wagged his great head slowly. 'No, they don't remove lower jaws like this and anyway, it shows no serious disease. And there's all the other bits of bone to consider.

'And of course, it's human?' Meredith wanted to keep the record straight, though he had no doubt of the answer.

Prosser grinned. 'I don't think even gorillas often get their teeth filled.'

Old Nick grunted. 'Right – so we've got a dead man to deal with. Now, what else can you tell me?' The forensic doctor took the jaw right out of the bag and studied it again after he had balanced his optical system on his nose.

'A young person, not a child, but probably between eighteen and twenty-five. One wisdom tooth is through, the other only half erupted. Some fillings, but a few bad cavities as well. Not careful about looking after his teeth, in other words.'

'The death – how recent was it?' persisted the chief-superintendent.

Prosser peered at him over his rims. 'Very difficult, very difficult!'

He had a strong North Wales accent, making the 'very' sound like 'ferry'. Peering again at the bone, he added grudgingly, 'There's burned tissue between the teeth. That means …' he hesitated in committing himself. Things said rashly were hard to retract later on. 'It could mean less than a year since death,' he wheezed.

The scientific officer, Roger Lewis, grinned and nudged his fat ribs.

'Come off it, Huw. That tissue has never been wetted since the fire. This is fresh, surely?'

Huw Prosser gave him a withering look. 'Not if it's been covered up,' he objected.

'Well it hasn't or the dog wouldn't have found it. And this particular ash has only been here since yesterday at the earliest.'

'Well, I didn't know that, did I?' muttered the doctor in an injured voice.

The whole party walked back to the edge of the tip and looked down the slope.

'If bones were tipped down there, the biggest bits would go the furthest,' observed the pathologist. 'So any whole bones like a skull or limb might actually be in the water.'

There was a silence as they digested the implications of this.

'That means pumping out the dock or using frogmen,' said Old Nick.

'They'd have to pump for bloody weeks,' observed Ellis gloomily. Although little of the dock was left, the actual volume of water was still massive.

The inspector's radio buzzed and he came across to Meredith with a message. 'The contractor has arrived at the Docks Station, sir.'

Old Nick sighed. 'Right, we'll go across, there's a lot of organizing to do. I've had bodies in all sorts of places in my time, but this one takes the prize.'

At six o'clock that Friday evening, a council of war was held in the Forensic Science Laboratory. This was a brand new building which nestled between the National Museum and the University in Cathays Park, the administrative centre of the capital.

In an upstairs room, the detectives and scientist sat solemnly around a large table on which were spread all the trophies to date from the West Dock.

On several large sheets of paper, a series of bone fragments were spread out, each one marked by a ticket giving the grid reference of the search area, which had been marked out with pegs and cord. Dr Huw Prosser had stopped wheezing now that he was settled on a chair.

‘Definitely a man – late teens or early twenties,’ he said ponderously. ‘He’d had dental treatment, but still neglected some bad cavities.’

Meredith brooded at the end of the table. Ellis looked up at him and thought he would have been a great hit in Victorian melodrama as the wicked squire.

‘This tooth neglect – is that any use for guessing at his social class?’ muttered Old Nick.

Prosser grimaced his doubts.

‘You’re as well-placed as I am to say that. On general grounds, I suppose a labourer is less careful of his teeth than say, a doctor or company executive. But there are so many exceptions that I wouldn’t let it influence you.’

He pulled at his ear and reassembled his broken train of thought.

‘The cause of death is absolutely unknown and will probably stay that way for ever. So far, after six hours scratching around, you’ve found forty-six bits of bone. Apart from the lower jaw, a bit of skull and the top of a thigh bone, they’ve all been splinters.’

Roger Lewis, the biologist, broke in.

‘I wonder why the jaw was so much less damaged by fire than the rest? It’s the only bit with any remains of tissue on it.’

The pathologist nodded. ‘The hinges are burnt, but the centre is only scorched, thank God … must have been out of the centre of the fire for some reason, otherwise it would have been calcined like the rest.’

‘What’s this “calcined” you keep talking about doc?’ asked Ellis.

‘Means that the bone is reduced to its mineral parts only – the fierce heat burns away the protein network, that’s why it’s so brittle.’ The pathologist answered with the earnestness of a professional teacher. Meredith was reminded of an aphorism of some ancient Greek – ‘More than the calf wants to suck, does the cow want to suckle.’

He grunted, one of his favourite sounds. 'No hope of knowing his height or anything else about him?'

Prosser smiled with polite deprecation.

'Not a chance, I'm afraid. One or two of these bits might be recognisable to an experienced anatomist, but there isn't a hope in hell of reconstructing the skeleton. We'd need at least a limb bone to have a shot at estimating the height.'

The chief superintendent sighed. 'No cause of death, no identity … some case I get landed with for my first Welsh murder!'

'Can't even say it's a murder,' murmured Prosser smoothly. 'Could be anything from coronary thrombosis to ingrowing toenails!'

'So how does he come to be unofficially cremated?' demanded Meredith. 'This is concealment of the body by a third person!'

Ellis idly wondered who the second person was, but wisely kept his thoughts to himself.

Lewis was staring at the fragments on the table.

'These bits are remarkably uniform in size, between one and two inches, mostly. If a chap fell accidentally into a fire, then you'd expect big bits and little bits left, even intact bones. There seems to have been deliberately bashed up to avoid notice.'

'Except the jaw and bits of skull,' observed Dai Rees, speaking for the first time.

'They must have been missed – a furnace big enough to take a whole body must have produced a lot of ash, easy to miss some pieces in that lot, especially if it had to be done on the sly or in a hurry,' agreed Prosser.

Meredith rasped fingers over his evening beard.

'That's the next thing. What sort of fire has he been in? Ellis, did you get all those details from the contractor?'

The detective inspector nodded and pulled a black

notebook from his pocket.

'Since yesterday, ashes were collected from five different places. Three of them use identical grades of fuel. The Coal Board chap said this afternoon that the ashes from the area of our bones must have come from this fuel – but he can't distinguish between the three.'

Old Nick chewed his fingers.

'You told me all that two hours ago – have we been around all those places where the ash comes from?'

'I've got lads out now, sir. Two of the furnaces were at factories on the docks and the other was a big office building just off James Street.'

Meredith looked back at the pathologist and the lab men.

'What's the next step as far as you're concerned?'

Prosser touched the jawbone gently with his pencil.

'This is the gem of the collection, the rest is just junk. With these fillings, you may well get a definite identity, if you can find the right dentist.'

Old Nick nodded brusquely. 'Have to hawk the details all round the city. How many dentists in Cardiff, I wonder?'

'Must be flaming scores of them,' said a heavy man sitting next to Meredith. This was Detective Chief Inspector Harris, Old Nick's senior assistant. He had been away all day at the Assizes and had only just come into the picture. The burden of organizing routine jobs such as dental searches fell on him; he was an anxious, worrying type and looked as if he didn't relish the idea.

'Try the Dental Hospital first,' he went on, 'then the local dentists in Butetown.'

'Of course, he may not be from Cardiff at all,' said Huw Prosser sweetly. 'Then you'll have a hell of a job on your hands … John o' Groats to Chipping Sodbury!'

Meredith looked sourly from the Job's comforter to Peter Wade. 'Any help you lab people can give us ?

You've had it soft so far.'

'Not with the bones,' answered the biologist, 'But if we get samples of boiler ash from these three places, we might be able to match one of them up with the stuff from around the bones.'

'But it was the same fuel in each case,' objected Ellis.

'Maybe, but different boilers may burn slightly differently. Design, temperature, draughts and all that, may make very slight differences in the nature of the ash. Worth trying, anyway.'

Old Nick got up, his lanky body towering above the table.

'I'll be glad if you can do that tonight, Mr Lewis. Ellis has the addresses of the places with the boilers. I'll be going around them myself later on, as soon as his scouts have reported back.'

The meeting broke up, the pathologist staying behind with the bones to make a provisional chart of the teeth.

In the morning, he intended getting expert advice from a dentist on the partly melted fillings and the age of the jaw, but to allow Harris's team to start chasing the dental records, he wanted to give them a rough diagram of the main features.

When the police officers reached their own headquarters on the other side of the park, the cadet on the reception desk buttonholed Bob Ellis.

'There's a chap to see you, sir, in the coroner's waiting room. He said it was urgent.'

A few minutes later Ellis broke in on Meredith, who was in his room organising details with Charlie Harris.

'Excuse me, sir, but think you ought to hear this, in case there's anything in it.' The reluctance in his voice suggested apology in advance for the waste of time. He stood aside to let a nervous, raincoated figure into the room.

‘This is Mr Price, sir – Iago Price. You remember, he runs an enquiry agency. Had a nasty accident a few days back, not far from the area we’re interested in.’

Ellis stumbled on, making half-excuses whilst Old Nick glared at him from under his beetling eyebrows.

Iago was sat in a chair facing the desk and Ellis felt sure that if he had brought a hat, he would have started twisting it around by the brim in the approved anxious manner.

‘Well?’ snapped Meredith, not laying much of a foundation for a nice cosy chat.

Iago cleared his throat and looked up at Bob Ellis, who was his anchor in this strange charade. He knew Charlie Harris as well, but there was a marked lack of sympathy between them. Ellis had always been more easy to get on with.

Meredith scowled across the desk and Iago hurriedly got his story under way.

‘I gather you already know about that car running Mr Summers and myself down the other night?’ he began diffidently. Meredith made a gargling sound; his frown stayed fixed in place.

‘I’m sure it was deliberate,’ Iago said desperately. ‘I’m lucky to have got off so lightly,’ This all seemed so much harder than when he had rehearsed it in front of his bathroom mirror.

‘I realize that you may not have had enough grounds to take it seriously, so I hired someone to do some private enquiries on my behalf.’

The prepared words sounded like rejected film script, but they got through to Old Nick.

‘You mean, you got someone to do your own snooping!’ he snapped impatiently. He didn’t know why this twerp was here at a hectic time like this. What was Ellis playing at?

‘I couldn’t go myself,’ countered Iago weakly. ‘I was

already known there. They'd had one go at me already!' Meredith looked over Price's head at Ellis. 'What's all this about, for God's sake?'

The detective inspector short-circuited Iago's laborious explanations.

'The chap he hired has gone missing, sir A fellow called Terry Rourke.'

Meredith's impatience vanished, but no one would have guessed it from his face. 'Rourke?' he repeated. 'Do we know him?'

'We do indeed,' answered Charlie Harris, who had a passion for remembering criminal records. 'Small-time yob, breakings and petty larceny. Spends most of his time on probation.'

Meredith looked down again at Iago.

'Go on, Mr Price.' The use of 'Mister' was a mark of acceptance.

'I saw him on Tuesday morning, paid him a retainer, and he went off to the Cairo Restaurant. I thought he might find some sign of damage on one of their cars or overhear something incriminating.'

'And did he?' demanded the chief superintendent.

'He telephoned the same night, said he had got a job as kitchen boy in the restaurant. I told him to ring back when he had something to tell me and he did so the next evening, quite late.'

Iago paused and swallowed hard. Suddenly, this visit to the fountainhead of detection didn't seem such a good idea. He faltered on.

'Rourke said he'd been eavesdropping outside Tiger Ismail's door, and he'd give it another day before packing up the job … that was the last I heard from him.'

'Wednesday night?' repeated Meredith tonelessly.

'Yes … I didn't hear from him all day Thursday. I was disappointed more than worried. Thought he'd just run out on the job. Then today I read about this body being found in the West Dock and got uneasy. I went over to Rourke's home in Riverside. His family haven't seen him since Wednesday, which is very unusual.'

He pulled a copy of the *South Wales Echo* from his raincoat pocket and tapped the front page headlines. 'When I saw this about it being the skeleton of a young man, I got really worried … probably nothing in it … thought I'd better just tell you '

His voice tailed off into an embarrassed mumble as he ran right out of self-confidence. He wished himself a mile away with his highly unlikely story.

But Meredith did not pour scorn on his head. He got up from his chair and stood stooping far above Iago's head.

'Thank you very much, Mr Price. As you say, probably nothing to worry about, but technically he's a missing person if his family is concerned about him. And we're interested in all missing persons in Cardiff, especially young men.'

He swung around to Harris. 'How old is this Rourke?'

'Twenty-three, twenty-four,' answered the other detective. 'Can check Records quick enough.'

Ellis nodded. 'He'd be about that. I wouldn't put too much store on him vanishing, though. He's a wild one, has about three jobs a week, when he's not sponging off the National Assistance.'

Meredith pierced Iago again with his dark eyes. 'Going back to the reason that you employed Rourke – did he find out anything for you?'

Iago shuffled uneasily on his chair. 'Not a lot – he said he'd come to the office next morning to give me details. That's partly why I got worried; he didn't turn up.'

The private detective thought it prudent not to mention that Terry had rifled Tiger's drawers and cupboards. 'He said that he had his ear to the door of an upstairs lounge and recognized the voice of a man called Davies, who was the one that approached Summers to blackmail him.'

Meredith nodded. He avoided saying that so far nothing of this could be substantiated by anyone but Iago himself.

'All he could hear was something about lorries on the Ross motorway, then someone else asked what the next job was.'

Iago was improvising here, but the general sense was right. 'Then Rourke heard a voice say "gaffer's chips on Sunday night".'

Ellis and Charlie Harris looked at each other. Lorries on the motorway made good sense to them after rumours about Tiger, but the rest was just gibberish. Meredith looked as if he was trying to decide if Iago was pulling their leg or headed for a padded cell.

'Gaffer's chips on Sunday night?' he echoed.

'Yes, exactly that. I wondered what the hell Rourke was talking about, so I got him to spell it out. I don't know what it meant,' he added unnecessarily.

There was a silence. The brief moment when Iago's credit seemed to have risen was over as 'gaffer's chips' was too much for them to swallow.

Meredith sniffed. 'Well, thank you, Mr Price. We'll look into this. I'm sure we'll turn up this Terry Rourke somewhere.'

They did turn up Terry Rourke, with the aid of a bulldozer. They eventually turned up a total of two hundred and seventeen fragments of him, but that was after he had been identified.

Later that evening, the Friday of the discovery of the jaw and of Iago's visit to police headquarters, a description of the teeth was printed and all available CID men were detailed to start going around dentists' surgeries next morning.

Their journey proved unnecessary, as that evening Detective Sergeant Willie Rees called at the Rourke household a mile from Bute Street. He did so halfheartedly, convinced that he was having his time wasted. Terry's mother, a rather vague, harassed woman in her fifties, answered the door of a terraced house that seemed to be bulging with children and young people.

Though she was worried by Terry's disappearance, she seemed to have so many other troubles that its importance was submerged. However, the sergeant gathered that it was unusual for her eldest son to spend a night away from home.

Rees tried not to alarm her too much. 'His last employer reported him absent from work – we're just checking up.'

He took down some mundane details in his notebook, then slipped in a casual question about Terry's dentist.

'Sure, I don't know, hardly ever did he go,' she. said with no apparent interest at this odd question. Luckily, one of the teenage sisters hanging about the background *could* tell him, and the sergeant made his exit after some comforting platitudes.

The dentist named was only a few streets away, but Rees could get no answer there at that time of the evening. Next morning, to get the loose ends tidied up before the real work began, he made it his first call.

He was 'on the knocker' at five past nine. By nine fifteen, he was hot-footing it back to Headquarters and at half past he was laying a buff dental record card on Meredith's desk. By noon the identity had been established beyond any doubt.

The dentist from Riverside, a lecturer from the dental college who specialized in such things, and the portly Dr Prosser had all sat in judgement on the jawbone, comparing it with the record card. They had declared it to be the jaw of Terry Rourke beyond all reasonable doubt and their provisional handwritten report lay on Meredith's desk.

It was there when he held a lunchtime conference with other senior officers. As well as Charlie Harris, Bob Ellis, and Willie Rees, there was present a new Detective Inspector to replace the one with the fractured arm, another DI from Headquarters, the uniformed Superintendent of 'A' Division, which included the Docks Station, and the deputy coordinator of the Regional Crime Squad.

Old Nick pushed his hands against his desk and rocked back dangerously on his chair.

'I've just had a word with the Chief about things. He's naturally anxious for us to pull out all the stops. The boffins have done a good quick job in getting an identity for us, so it's up to us now to equal them by some snappy police work.'

He shot a dark look at Bob Ellis. 'How are you getting on with this furnace angle?'

Bob pushed himself off a filing cabinet and almost stood to attention.

'The forensic people have been to see each of the three possible boilers this morning, sir. They phoned just now to say that we can eliminate one of the factories straight away – a totally different kind of ash from the other two, which seem to be indistinguishable from each other. Both use identical makes of boiler and though they're still working on it, they can't tell the ash apart.'

'Which two are these?'

'One is in the office building on the corner of Tydfil Street, the other is in a furniture factory in Dumballs Road. The office block is an old one, got all sorts of firms in it, shipping companies, the lot.'

Old Nick gnawed at the edges of his nails. 'Have your lads found anything significant to favour one place or the other?'

Ellis shrugged. 'Both have got pretty lax routines at night. Almost anybody could have got at the furnaces. At the factory, the furnace is in full view of the working area, so that seems to rule out anyone bunging in a body during working hours. They don't have a night shift.'

'What about the night, then?'

'The boiler is damped down and the nightwatchman comes out a few times to bung a bit of coke on. Security is awful there; there could easily have been a break-in if someone wanted to get at the furnace.'

Meredith looked shrewdly at the detective inspector. 'You're keeping the best till last – you favour the other place?'

Ellis nodded. 'The boiler is in the basement, not kept locked in the daytime. Anyone could get in by just walking down the steps from the street. There's a full-time boiler-cum-maintenance man in the daytime. He spends a lot of time in the basement next to the boiler room, but he goes up into the offices a lot to do odd jobs.'

'Again, what about the night?'

'The day chap knocks off at six, then an old fellow takes over until next morning. He feeds the boiler, makes tea and shuffles round the building with a torch every now and then.' Ellis coughed to conceal his satisfaction at the coming punchline 'He's an Arab, sir!'

There was an almost palpable silence as the policemen chewed this one over in their minds. The implication was obvious.

'Has he coughed anything?' asked Harris harshly.

Ellis made a face. 'No, he's as old as hell, stone-deaf into the bargain. I slipped around myself to see him when the boys brought in the news. Couldn't get a thing out of him. He's either a bit senile, a bit daft or just plain cunning. Pretends either not to hear you or not to understand you!'

Meredith's blue cheeks seemed to cave in even more under the harsh light of the bare room.

'The "lab" are definite that it must be one of these two furnaces, eh?'

'That's where the ash was collected from these past two days,' said Ellis defensively.

'Then we'll have to grind this old feller down a bit – where can we get hold of him in the daytime?'

'He lives in digs a couple of streets away from the offices.'

'No known connection with Tiger Ismail?'

'Nothing we know of, so far,' replied Bob Ellis cautiously. 'But after a couple of generations of inbreeding down there, I'll bet his second son's wife's sister's cousin is an Ismail!'

'Doesn't have to mean anything,' objected the 'A' division superintendent. 'The bulk of our residents – Arab, Greek, Indian – anything – they're as straight as the rest of Cardiff. Straighter than many!' he added with aggressive defence of his local flock.

Meredith raised a hand placatingly. For all his gloomy brusqueness, he knew when to play it soft.

'I know, I know, some of the biggest villains are up in the stockbroker belt. But we've got to eliminate the obvious.'

'We've got nothing on Tiger, anyway,' Charlie Harris reminded them. 'Only long-term suspicions and some hare-brained claptrap from that idiot Price.'

The mention of the enquiry agent triggered off Old Nick. His head jerked up towards Ellis. 'Have you got that fellow for me?.I'd better be having a few more words with him, I think,'

The inspector nodded. 'I've told him to be at Bute Street Station at half two this afternoon.'

Several of the soccer fans present groaned inwardly – it was Saturday and the City were playing at home that afternoon.

Meredith made a quick round-up of all the straggling threads.

'Summers, the man from the bank. Anything new?'

‘Still the same,’ supplied Harris. ‘Deeply unconscious and likely to remain so, for all the Infirmary can tell.’ Meredith thought rapidly. ‘Better treat that running-down as a serious crime now. A bit late, but see if you can get Summers’ clothing from the hospital. We’ll get them up to the lab in case there’s any paint flakes and all that rigmarole.’

He gobbled his finger, then shot a look at Willie Rees.

‘Check at the Docks end. Snoop around any car associated with the Cairo Restaurant. Check garages and accident repair yards. Put somebody on to stolen car lists for the period that interests us. You know the drill as well as I do,’ he ended impatiently.

Having ordered in a couple of sentences enough work for half the City CID for a week, Meredith jumped to something else.

‘What are we going to do about this guy Ismail – has anyone approached him yet?’

‘Waiting for you to say, sir,’ said Ellis, with a questioning look across at Charlie Harris. They were still feeling their way with Meredith, they didn’t know yet whether he was the sort who wanted all the reins in his own hand or if he wanted people to use their own heads. Both ways had their peculiar advantages and dangers. Ellis was particularly vulnerable. He had been thrown into the case from the start, before it had escalated into a five-star crime. He had to be wary of treading on several senior toes.

Meredith solved his problem.

‘I’ll do it myself,’ he growled. ‘But I want to talk to Price first.’ He glowered around the room, even at the Crime Squad man, who was the same rank as himself. Although they had only known Old Nick a few weeks, already it was apparent that his satisfaction was inversely proportional to the depth of his scowl.

‘Any questions?’ he challenged.

Harris had one. 'What about this motorway stuff and "gaffer's chips" rubbish?'

Old Nick looked towards the Crime Squad man.

'The lorry hijacking might be something for you. As for the other, they were probably talking about the menu in the cafe. If you can think of a criminal explanation, I'll be glad to hear it!'

On this sarcastic note, the conference broke up.

Chapter Seven

Several other meetings were going on at the same time, all within a mile or so of police headquarters.

In the Glendower Arms, Iago Price and Dilys were hunched over a couple of hot pies and half pints. Unlike their sessions each evening, they were in the thick of a Saturday lunchtime crowd of drinkers and Lewis Evans had little time to join them in their discussion of the recent drama.

'I jus' can't believe it!' said the blonde for the fourth time. 'He can't be dead – not murdered! He was patting my bottom only a couple of days ago.'

Iago was too preoccupied to listen to her, he was wondering about a recent phone message from Ellis.

'It must be that, Dilys. Why else should I get an urgent call to meet the chief superintendent at half-past two? It means they've identified the body and want to grill me a lot further.'

'What's this Meredith like?' she asked curiously.

'Real grim character,' muttered Iago. 'Scares the pants off me. He'd break his face if he smiled; he looks like an old-time chapel preacher. Wears a long black coat and a hat that was made about nineteen twenty-nine! … but they say he's hot stuff at his job.'

Dilys prodded the remains of her pie dispiritedly. 'But we don't know that's what he wants you for. It may be about the running-down, perhaps they've found the car. I can't believe that boy is dead!'

Iago gulped, his outsize Adam's apple bobbing like a yo-yo.

‘Look, somebody’s dead and it’s more likely to be Terry Rourke than anyone else. Burnt skeletons don’t just appear spontaneously in the West Dock.’

Lewis Evans came across to pull a handful of halves. As he worked the old fashioned pumps, he whispered hoarsely across the bar.

‘Any definite news yet?’ He felt responsible for introducing Terry to Iago and was anxious to get the rumours either allayed or confirmed.

Iago made him up to date with what news there was.

The banging of empty glasses on the other end of the bar cut short any more chat, but Iago felt Dilys’ hand on his arm and nearly fell off the stool with ecstasy.

‘Can you get into trouble with the police for sending Terry to spy on these people?’ she asked, with genuine anxiety in her voice.

Iago glowed, even through his troubles, at the sympathetic change in her manner.

‘Can’t see how,’ he replied. ‘He wasn’t breaking any law down there. I didn’t tell the police that he said he’d broken open some drawers and a desk. And it doesn’t matter now, if he’s dead,’ he ended, rather bitterly.

The girl squeezed his arm.

‘It wasn’t your fault, Iago … every time you send me to the post office I could get run over, but that doesn’t make you responsible, does it?’

Iago smiled wanly at her, not far from tears of mixed self-pity and gratitude at her sympathy. His moustache seemed to wilt and a latent, if unsuspected, maternal feeling began to stir deep inside Dilys.

He sighed and looked up at the clock.

'Time I was going, allowing for Lewis’s bar time. Will I see you later on?’

She nodded. ‘I’ll do a bit of shopping, then come back to the office by four. You can buy me a cuppa and tell me all about it.’

She smiled encouragingly as she left him and, for a moment, a bright shaft of anticipation broke through his gloom. Yet even the prospect of making headway with Dilys was sour success if it depended on Rourke's death.

Iago hurried out of the bar and made for the top of Bute Street. As he walked along the worn pavements, past sleazy cafes and abandoned shops, his mood began to change.

He accepted the fact that the police were going to tell him that the body was that of his late employee and as he did so, his self-reproach began to turn to slow anger. With the anger came frustration that a mob of criminals could run down two men in a city street and then eliminate a harmless youth, all with apparent impunity.

He quickened his step as his temper began to smoulder. Passing over the hump of the old canal bridge, the straight line of Bute Street stretched away almost to the horizon. Like a child's perspective drawing, the grey railway embankment wall on his left and the motley collection of old buildings on the other side converged in the distance.

A row of police cars stood outside the police station, blue and white Pandas, a white traffic wagon and two black patrol cars. Nearby, the pneumatic drills and bulldozers were silent against their backcloth of rubble and half demolished buildings. On a Saturday, with the City playing at home, the population had drained away westwards to Ninian Park.

Iago looked at his watch and walked through the uninviting doors dead on two thirty. A sergeant answered his knock on the Enquiries hatch and took him through the dismal corridors to the CID room.

'Mr Price, sir.' The uniformed officer tapped on the door and left him with three men he already knew.

Meredith was the centrepiece, black overcoat and all. The chief superintendent pointed to a vacant chair and Iago sat down. The slow anger still burned and he felt none of his usual diffidence.

He gazed at Meredith's hawk-like face noticing for the first time the grey at the sides of his otherwise black, lank hair.

'Mr Price, I'm afraid we'll have to take you over all that you've told us before in greater detail.' He motioned briefly towards Ellis and Rees who stood at either side, then his eyes fixed on Iago again as if daring him to tell anything but the whole truth.

'I'm afraid your fears yesterday were well-founded. The body *was* that of Terence Rourke. The teeth proved it beyond any doubt.'

He paused to let this sink well in. Although Iago had already resigned himself to the fact of Terry's death, Meredith's words made him go cold inside. He swallowed hard a few times and for some reason felt acutely sick.

Meredith waited, then continued as if nothing had happened. He had found from bitter experience that fussing with the soft approach usually made things worse. Anyway, it was Mrs. Rourke who was due for any sympathy. If it wasn't for this silly, interfering amateur sitting here, Rourke would still be alive. *Or would he*? That was what Meredith was paid to find out.

'You told me the outline last night. I want to fill in with every detail you can remember. Firstly, is there anything in the Summers part of the affair that you haven't told me?'

Iago, still white and quivery, thought for a moment, then said there was not.

In spite of this, Old Nick went over the whole story again, patiently enlarging on every point and probing every angle. Dai Rees unobtrusively kept a note of what was said, as he would have to go through Iago's old statement later on and build any additional information into a supplementary one.

Meredith pulled his own notebook from a pocket. It was not a standard police issue, but a thick one with a glossy cover, black like the rest of him.

He scowled through the pages, then asked, 'This woman Betty. Summers never managed to get a line on her?'

Iago shook his head.

'I asked him that. When he went back to her flat, she had cleared out, no forwarding address. The details she gave to the bank about her employment were all phoney too, even her Insurance card.'

Meredith looked up at Ellis, then at Rees. 'Anyone on the fringes of the Ismail outfit who might fit her description?'

The two detectives looked at one another, then shook their heads.

'Their "fringe" is so big, we don't know half of them, sir,' said Rees, 'But no one springs to mind. Though surely, wouldn't they have used a girl outside the immediate clan, just to avoid being traced?'

Meredith grunted. 'What's Tiger's reputation with women?' he demanded.

'Opinions vary, sir,' replied Ellis. 'He's a bachelor and very much the lone wolf. Dresses a bit fancy, but that's nothing to go by these days. Some reckon he's "queer", but that's a load of rubbish.'

Nicholas Meredith scratched something in his notebook with a small pencil, then turned back to Iago Price.

'You said the only contact Terry Rourke had with you was a phone call on the evening of Wednesday. Do you know where he phoned from?

'A call box – definitely. He didn't say where it was, but he'd just knocked off work in the restaurant, so it must have been nearby.'

Meredith scribbled some more and glanced up at Harris long enough to say, 'Check all the boxes in the area for signs of a fight.'

To Iago he said, 'I want you to remember all the details

of what he told you … I know you've done it twice before, but this is vitally important now. Any details, no matter how damn silly they may sound.'

Iago thought hard. This matter-of-fact approach was good for his state of mind, it stopped him wallowing in self-recrimination. He tried to throw his mind back to the night when Terry had spoken to him on the telephone.

'He said he'd just left the Cairo Restaurant – told me he'd had a bit of luck, but couldn't see much future in carrying on there. Then he said he'd had the chance to look in Tiger's rooms and have a glance at some of his papers.'

Old Nick's head snapped up. 'You didn't tell us this before!'

Iago's pallor flushed into pinkness. 'I must have forgotten that,' he mumbled. 'Rourke said he'd opened the doors of Ismail's lounge and bedroom and looked through all the drawers. He opened a locked desk too, but there was nothing there he could recognize as incriminating in any way.'

'Anything else?' rumbled the senior detective, his long face glowering at Iago.

'There was a safe there, though he didn't attempt cracking that,' faltered Iago. 'Apart from that, it's exactly as I told you. Something about lorries on the Ross Motorway – the M50, I suppose – then this bit about "gaffer's chips on Sunday".'

'Who else was in the restaurant?'

'He mentioned Florrie, Tiger's aunt and an Uncle Ahmed. He said he'd seen Joe Davies in there, and some others, but he didn't say who.'

'Do the names Archie Vaughan or Nikos Kalvos mean anything to you?'

The enquiry agent shook his head, then thought of something else.

'The night Summers and I were run down, there was a chap near us in the Glendower Arms. The landlord says he seemed to be eavesdropping on us, then he suddenly got up and went, even left his drink behind. A few minutes later, we were bowled over by that car!'

'What was he like?'

'I didn't notice him, but the barman says he was very thin and small, like a jockey,'

'Archie Vaughan!' said Rees and Ellis simultaneously. Iago felt a throb of righteous pleasure in his breast as at last something confirmed his story, of which the police seemed so sceptical.

Meredith showed no such satisfaction. Head down, he said, 'See the barman, Rees, get a statement. Got any photographs of these merchants yet?'

Dai Rees had his own notebook out.

'Not yet, we're chasing Records for them. Almost all this crowd have got form, so we should be all right for a picture of most of them.'

Old Nick grunted. 'Get a photo, show it to Mr Price here. Then go around to the landlord of that pub. See if they can pick out Vaughan, for a start.'

'Right, I'll have one of Rourke printed, too, we may need a general search for anyone who saw him on Wednesday or Thursday.'

Old Nick went back to trying to squeeze any last drops of information out of Iago Price. It was soon clear that he was now as dry as any stone. Soon Meredith got up, his height making the little room seem tiny, especially with the other large officers in there as well.

'Thank you for your help, Mr Price. Anything else that might come back to you will be very welcome. We'll just get all that down in another formal statement and you can go.'

He cleared his throat and altered the pitch of his voice to make it more severe. 'I have to say now that you did a very unwise thing in employing Rourke on what was frankly a quite illegal job. You weren't to know the outcome, I suppose, but his breaking and entering Ismail's rooms was bad. It might have involved you in conspiring to commit a felony or whatever the new Act calls it now. But in the unfortunate circumstances, we'll forget that. I'd stick to divorce work in the future, if I were you.'

This was the dismissal and with a murmured farewell Iago slunk away after Rees to make his statement in another room. Half an hour later, he left the station in a subdued mood and made his way back through the ghosts of old Tiger Bay.

Meredith and Bob Ellis had their own cars parked in a side street near the police station – or what had been a side street, now just a tarmac strip between rubble and new foundations.

Ellis was going with Old Nick to interview the watchman at the office block, so far the most likely source of the bones. He led the way from Bute Street in his Hillman, with Meredith – a stranger to these more obscure parts of the city – following in his Austin 1800.

As he kept behind the Hillman, Nicholas Meredith allowed himself a few rare moments of introspection. For the first time since leaving London, he took stock of himself in his new role in life.

How odd, he thought, that returning to his native land seemed a bigger wrench than leaving twenty-two years earlier. Not an unpleasant wrench, but certainly an upheaval.

For six years and more since he had been a superintendent at the Yard, he had had the itch to come home. When the chance had arrived he almost funked it, afraid of himself and the possibility of a let-down when he exchanged the known for the unknown.

For years, Wales had loomed larger and larger in his dreams. Every holiday was spent there, even snatched weekends. The prospect of 'going home' had become almost an obsession, but when the chance actually came, he found himself frightened. Not of anything tangible, but fear of disillusion, the fear that the reality wouldn't live up to the dream.

Two months later he was still walking this tightrope, waiting for a sign to tell him whether he had done the right thing. This case, the first killing, would probably provide the sign. He didn't know how yet, but he felt it deep inside.

As a murder, it was nothing outstanding. Intriguing and unusual perhaps, especially by Cardiff standards, though twenty years in the 'Met' had made him incapable of thinking in capital letters about any crime.

But this was going to be the first big case for Nicholas Meredith – 'Old Nick', as he well knew they were calling him already.

He was the CID boss here – in the Smoke, however blasé he could afford to be about big-time crime, he had been only one superintendent amongst scores. He thought wryly about the old saw of the 'big fish and the little pond'.

Yet Cardiff was a big city – a capital city – and it had plenty of crime relative to its population. On paper it had a higher crime rate than London. Newcastle was top of the league and Cardiff was about third, with London well down the list. He snorted to himself as he thought that statistics could prove anything. Stealing bicycles was equivalent to mass murder in the Home Office crime figures.

He sighed as he halted behind Ellis's Minx at a set of traffic lights. He watched the other car's traffic indicator winking to turn right and thought that this place was as foreign to him as Hong Kong, though he was born only forty miles away.

The brick-and-mortar forests of Hackney, Bayswater and the West End had become more familiar to him than his home town of Swansea, though Hitler had taken a big hand in re-shaping the streets of his boyhood. Cardiff was quite strange to him – like so many Welshmen, the only part he knew was the Arms Park Rugby Ground, and a dozen public houses nearby.

Though Meredith's thoughts centred on the changes in his surroundings, he failed to see that his own character raised the biggest barrier to acceptance.

He genuinely had no idea of how remote he could be. He consciously kept his staff at a distance, sincerely believing that familiarity weighed against efficiency. He craved for acceptance by his men, but was determined not to buy it with easy bonhomie-like slaps on the back, Christian names and pints in the local after every case. He stuck grimly to his role of 'The Boss', expecting respect to come from the results of hard work on the part of all the team, not least his own hard work.

His slight eccentricities in dress were no gimmick; he genuinely never noticed his outdated clothes. His good-natured, but rather vague wife occasionally made feeble protests about his appearance, but these he impatiently brushed off as 'women's nagging'.

As he followed the Hillman on the last lap of the short journey, he wondered how eager the 'Met' had been to get rid of him. Often the enthusiasm of testimonials was inversely proportional to a man's popularity, so that there would be a better chance of unloading him on to someone else!

He had certainly walked into the job against all competition and promptly began worrying about whether it was due to his undoubted success as a thief-taker or his being a square peg in a round London hole!

His self-examination was cut short by the winking of Ellis's tail lights. The detective inspector had pulled up outside a high, old-fashioned office block which stood on the corner of a side street.

The weak winter daylight was already fading, but Meredith could see the ornate frescoes around the entrance and the intricate stonework of the window mullions – a reminder of the affluent days of the coal boom when prestige and profits were reflected in the pseudo-classical efforts of Victorian and Edwardian architects.

The heavy oak doors at the top of the front steps were tightly closed, but Ellis led him around the corner into Tydfil Street. Here another much smaller flight of steps led down from the pavement. They clattered down the iron treads to a door at the bottom, about twelve feet below street level.

Ellis banged on the faded panels and shouted, 'Harry! Police again.'

Meredith looked at him in the gloom of the stairwell.

'Harry? I thought this chap was an immigrant?'

'Proper name is Arif bin Pandek – so everyone calls him "Harry".'

'Funny name for an Arab.'

'Got a dash of Malay in him, I think.' Ellis grunted.

He banged on the door again and eventually there was the sound of shuffling feet and rusty bolts being drawn.

'You said this place was open day and night,' said Old Nick, accusingly.

'It was until today. I had a word with the owners, who have the whole of the ground floor offices. The manager did his nut, came dashing down with orders for the boilerman to keep the place locked up in future.'

The door opened slowly and a face like a leather gargoyle peered out. The high cheekbones were covered in wrinkled brown skin that caved in where the back teeth should have been. A sunken, gummy mouth quivered at them.

'Policemen?' it croaked.

Ellis pushed the door open and stood back for Meredith to enter.

‘Remember me, Harry? I was here this morning. This is the chief policeman. He wants to ask you more questions.’

All this had to be said over again at double volume, as Arif appeared to be almost stone-deaf.

They worked their way into a large room that was part-workshop and part-bedroom. A bench with a vice and a collection of rusty tools occupied one half, while a table and camp bed shared the other part with a small gas stove and an antiquated radio set.

The table carried milk bottles, half a loaf and some dirty crockery, which overflowed onto a cracked porcelain sink and draining board in the corner.

Harry tramped behind them on painful feet to sit on the edge of the grubby bed, one hand cupped ready about his left ear. Meredith saw that he wore a length of cloth wound round his head, a brown storekeeper’s coat and a pair of ex-navy bell-bottoms which flapped around his skinny ankles.

‘Where is the boiler?’ shouted Old Nick. At the second attempt, the message got through and the old man waved a hand at an open door opposite the workbench.

Meredith and Ellis walked through and looked around them. They saw a much larger room with a flight of steps going up to the ground floor. A forest of pipes and valves came from a large boiler against an adjacent wall. It looked as if it had been taken from a ship the size of the *Mauretania*, complete with brass fittings and pressure gauges. The rest of the room was half-filled with coke, which was overflowing from a steel hatch in the opposite wall.

Ellis pointed at this. ‘There’s a big bunker behind there, sir. Must hold all of fifty tons. It’s filled from a manhole in the street.’

Meredith looked around critically. ‘Any other way in, except the steps we came down?’

‘No, except from the offices, down those other stairs.

There's the ash lift, of course, but that can only be worked from inside here.'

The chief superintendent looked more closely at the boiler. The firebox was set on a massive concrete foundation and had a steel fire door about two feet square. This had large strap hinges riveted on to the front and a long lever which dropped into a slot to keep it shut.

Old Nick walked briskly across to it, raising a black dust from the floor as he went. He gingerly felt the end of the lever, but it was no more than comfortably warm. Lifting it, he pulled the fire door open and bent to look inside. He saw a long cavern, at least six feet deep, glowing dully at the edges.

'Banked down for the weekend, sir,' volunteered the inspector. 'I saw it this morning when it was going full blast, You could hardly bear to look inside then.' Meredith slammed the door shut.

'Plenty of room in there for a body. What happens to the ashes?'

Ellis pointed to a steel plate running the length of the base.

'That's the edge of a big metal box – it pulls out and runs on castors to that lift over there.'

On the outside wall of the basement was a crude lift operated by a chain hoist. 'It goes up on that into a big hopper at the top. There's a chute from there into the lorries, which come to empty it every couple of days.'

They had a last look around the room, then went back to where Arif was sitting patiently on his bed.

Meredith bawled into his ear. 'When did they last empty the ashes?'

The old Arab turned his calm brown eyes on the detectives and shrugged.

'I do not know, sir. The day shift man, he does that.'

'Doesn't know nothing, this old bugger!' muttered Ellis. The old man's eyes flicked sharply towards him.

Meredith tried again. 'Until today, the door was always open, eh?'

He struck oil here.

Arif nodded. 'Always! Sometimes my friends, they come in at night to take tea and talk. I got no enemies,' he added enigmatically.

'Anyone else been in this week, except your friends?'

This took a second bellowing to get through, then Arif shook his head.

'No one at all?' barked Meredith.

This high-decibel interrogation went on for some time. All the nightwatchman's friends were listed, but Arif bin Pandek admitted to no events out of the ordinary during the past few nights. Meredith found his stonewalling infuriating; usually an astute judge of a witness, this Asiatic impassiveness threw all his usual criteria right off-centre. Old Nick knew that the fellow was either being truthful, cunning, or lying – or was just plain dim – but he couldn't tell which it was.

Harry did admit to being out of the basement for at least an hour every night.

'I am so old, sir, and so slow now. I take many minutes to get upstairs, my feet are so bad. I have to look in every room for fire, so I am away from here a long time every night.'

He didn't actually say it, but the inference was that if any funny business had been going on in his basement, it must have been when he was away on his rounds.

Meredith gave up eventually and turned to Ellis. 'Do you known definitely when the last ash collection was made from here?' he demanded.

'Yesterday, about nine o'clock in the morning.'

'And before that?'

'Beginning of the week – Monday.' Bob Ellis had it off pat.

'So if the bones came from here, it must have been just

before they were found in the dock?'

He turned to look at the patient watchman. 'Has he made a formal statement?'

'Rees took it today. Said exactly what he's told you. Damn all!'

Old Nick rasped a finger over his stubble. 'Better take the ash that's accumulated since yesterday. Arrange for it to be collected and sent up to the forensic lab. There may be something still left that will tie it in with the bones. One bit would be enough for us.'

Leaving the ancient Arab to his lonely vigil, they made their way back to the cars.

'Hard to tell if he's shooting us a line, sir.' Ellis tried to break through the heavy silence that had come down like a curtain over Meredith.

The senior man grunted in reply.

'Have to get on the knocker round these streets, Ellis. All these houses, see if they heard anything unusual on Wednesday night or Thursday morning.' He waved a hand at the rows of small terraced houses that made up Tydfil Street.

Ellis nodded, then stopped hesitantly with his hand on the door of his Hillman.

'Where now, sir? Back to the station?'

Meredith straightened his black hat carefully.

'No, I think the time has come to meet this Tiger,' he said softly.

Chapter Eight

An hour later the opposition were having their own council of war.

Joe Davies, glass in hand and feet propped on a coffee table, looked smug and confident. 'You handled them like a genius, Tiger … that dark, miserable sod looked fit to hand in his badge when he was leaving.'

His confidence cut no ice with Ismail, who stood restlessly near the window, staring down into the street below. He swung round on Joe, a glare of anger on his usually impassive face.

'If it wasn't for you brainless set of bastards, there would have been no need for this Meredith and his mob to have come here in the first place,' he said in a biting snarl. 'First that fool of a Greek with his car, then you … after this, I'm packing up, d'you hear! I'm starting from scratch, with a bunch of boys I can trust to do what I tell them.'

Joe flushed and half rose from the chair. He thought better of it and sank back, taking a wallet from his pocket.

'Look, Tiger, we had to rub him out, di'n't we?' he appealed. 'He'd been on the snoop in here. God knows what he heard. Look at these!' He held out two pieces of paper, but Ismail ignored them. Joe put them on the table and smoothed them out. 'I told you, Tiger, Terry Rourke was planted on us. Here's a cheque for fifteen quid signed by that bloody stupid private dick … and here's a sheet of paper in your handwriting.'

Ismail strode across and snatched it from Joe's hand, throwing it into the hearth. 'I told you, that's only some rough accounts from the cafe.'

Joe Davies wagged his head knowingly. 'But it shows he went rooting through your papers, don't it! In his wallet, these were, when we done him.'

Tiger whirled away scornfully. 'When you done him!' he mimicked with a sneer. 'Listen, we're small-time thieves, not Al Capone. We've made a packet of money these past couple of years and not done a day's bird for it. We haven't made a million, but at least we've stayed outside the nick where we could enjoy the loot. Now you and the other BFs go and louse it all up by playing gangsters!'

Joe started to protest his innocence, but Tiger, without raising his voice, steamrollered him by sheer force of personality. 'Look, get it into your head that your level is knocking off trucks and a bit of smuggling. Even that bank idea you had was out of our class – it was that that dropped us right in it this time!'

Davies muttered something under his breath and scowled into his drink. Archie Vaughan and Nikos Kalvos sat quietly, trying to look inconspicuous. Though they looked like naughty schoolboys, their naughtiness had led to a manslaughter charge hanging over them, possibly even murder.

Like the affair with the car, it had been a case of misplaced enthusiasm. When Terry Rourke came downstairs after his snooping, he was wrong in thinking that his exploits had gone unnoticed. Uncle Ahmed, who was by no means as senile as he looked, had padded up the stairs after him and heard him searching in Tiger's lounge.

When Joe and the others came down later, Uncle had told them about Rourke. Joe had rushed out into the night after Terry and caught up with him at the phone box just as the Irish boy was finishing his call to Iago Price. When the others caught up they formed the grim reception committee for Rourke as he stepped from the box. Joe got the proceedings off to a good start by punching Terry in the mouth and the interview took that line from then on. They dragged him to a nearby alley and, in spite of a spirited defence, the three men pounded him into a stupor. They got no word of confession mixed with his rapidly weakening blasphemies.

When he lay almost senseless on the cobbles, Joe Davies went through his pockets and triumphantly discovered the cheque and other papers from Tiger's desk. With this proof of Rourke's villainy, Joe decided to take him back to Tiger to see what was to be done. As he bent to pick him off the ground, the foxy Irishman brought a knee up to smash into Joe's groin. With a quick twist, he was up and away, dashing for the open street at the end of the alley.

In a blind rage of pain and anger, Davies – almost twice the size of Terry – pounded after him. He caught his victim within a few yards and grabbed him around the throat with a grip like a gorilla.

At the sudden impact of thumb and fingers on both carotid arteries, Terry Rourke crumpled to the ground like an empty sack.

When they tried to pick him up, they found that he was quite dead.

'You done for 'im, Joe!' whispered Archie, hoarsely. They stared aghast at the twisted shape on the ground.

Uncle Ahmed, a late starter and a slow runner, caught them up and gazed down expressionlessly at the body. He alone had the sense to do something quickly. 'Policeman come along soon – better get him home to the cafe,' he said simply. 'Pretend he is drunken.'

Joe, his anger evaporated by the turn of events, nodded dully. He and Nikos, the other heavyweight, grabbed Terry on either side and they tried to imitate a party limping home after a heavy night on the beer. The charade was strained and cheerless, but their luck held and they went through the back lanes to the Cairo Restaurant without seeing a soul.

Leaving the body in an outhouse they went up to Tiger's room to tell him the bad news.

His cold, seething anger was worse than a violent rage, but his inbred fatalism rapidly brought him around to practical matters.

'Sure he's dead, you damn fools?' he hissed.

Joe nodded miserably. He was grey and sweating with delayed shock. He had many a wounding and 'grievous bodily harm' to his credit, but a killing was new to him.

Ismail pulled on a suede jacket. 'Wait here – I'm going round to see someone.'

Taking the old uncle, he drove his Zodiac to within a few hundred yards of the Compass Building in Tydfil Street. Dropping Ahmed off, he drove well away and came back in ten minutes to pick up the old man again. Uncle Ahmed reported that Arif, his second cousin, was on duty in the basement as usual and had taken the hint to be out of the way for the next half hour, with no questions asked.

Tiger drove back to Bute Street and garaged the car. A few minutes later an old Morris station wagon, belonging to yet another distant member of the family, was on the road. It stopped for a couple of seconds at the basement steps of the office building, sufficient time for Joe Davies and the Greek to slide down the steps with a long bundle wrapped in sacking. Ten minutes later, the two men walked back to the main road to be picked up by the cruising Morris. It was now well after midnight and there was no one to notice the black smoke that drifted for a time high over the Compass building.

Since that Wednesday night, Tiger had gone over every detail of the affair in his mind a hundred times. So far he could find no flaw, apart from the unlikely chance of someone peering through their windows for a brief moment in the middle of the night – someone who would have to have super-cat's eyes in that gloom. The only real flaw had been the great one of having the murder discovered at all and the even more tragic one of having the police tracing it back to the Compass Building so quickly.

Though this was a setback of the first order, he still felt that they were safe enough. Uncle Ahmed had told his cousin to spend all night breaking up anything he could find in the furnace with a cleaning rod. The old fool must have missed the jawbone and knocked it through the fire-bars into the ash pan. He had been instructed to look through the ashes as well, and destroy any recognizable pieces, but evidently this was easier said than done. 'You think old Arif will be copper-proof?' asked Joe now.

Tiger glared at him coldly. 'If you do half as well, we'll be all right. My family stick together – and *think* before they do crazy things!' he retorted acidly.

He paced up and down the thick carpet. He was not worried about the nightwatchman's tongue wagging – he could put on his deaf and dumb act for eternity. It was *this* mob here that worried him.

The police had spent almost an hour at the Cairo this evening. Thankfully, only Tiger and the cafe staff were there. Meredith expected – and drew – a complete blank from everyone. No one had heard anything, seen anything or knew anything about anything!

Yes, Terry Rourke had worked there for a day and a half. He had gone off on Wednesday night as usual and had not been seen since. They knew his feckless reputation and were not a bit surprised.

Meredith, with the intuition of years of interviewing behind him, knew it was waste of time trying any clever methods of interrogation on them. This bunch were as close as any Mafiosi and had the added veneer of the East to deter any questioner.

He admitted to Tiger that he had no warrant, but asked to see over the premises. Ismail readily agreed and with a certain sense of futility, Meredith and Ellis tramped through every room and looked in every cupboard.

Then they went away, to think of something else to do.

At ten o'clock Nicholas Meredith called it a day and left headquarters for home. He drove slowly back to his home at Lakeside, in the northern part of the city thinking all the way of the various unsatisfactory angles of his first killing in Wales.

It seemed impossible to think otherwise than that Ismail's mob must be responsible for Rourke's death.

If Iago Price were to be believed, then there was a definite threat of events touching the owner of the Cairo Restaurant at several points. The running-down of Price and Summers – if it was no accident – followed close on Joe Davies's encounter with Summers at the Red Dragon public house and on the odd behaviour of a man almost certain to be Archie Vaughan. Even now, Ellis and Rees were looking for the other members of Ismael's clique to interview them, but Meredith had little doubt that they would have ready-made stories to cover their movements.

As he drove sedately past the large lake in Roath Park, he wondered how much he could rely on Iago's story about Terry Rourke's last phone call. All that mumbo-jumbo about 'gaffer's chips' seemed too puerile to be imagination and was perhaps all the more credible as a result.

Certainly, Rourke had gone to the cafe to work. Tiger Ismail admitted that freely … and Iago Price had a counterfoil in his chequebook to show that he had paid Rourke a retainer, so that appeared to tie up the truth of the whole over-dramatic affair.

But there, the trail of evidence ended abruptly. Ismail said that Rourke had left work on Wednesday night and hadn't been back … in the absence of any other evidence, that was Full Stop Number One.

Then the body had almost certainly been disposed of in the Compass Building – *the furniture factory was far less likely*, thought Meredith, as he swung his Austin into the new estate where he lived.

The last pointer was that a relative of Tiger was on duty at a time when the body was almost certainly cremated – old Arif's relationship to the Ismail clan had just been unearthed by Detective Sergeant Rees. Although this sounded promising at the start, it was really about as much evidential value as a puff of smoke. Tiger had lost no time in pointing out that at least a hundred people in Cardiff's dockland were related to him as closely as old Pandek. And as the old man himself steadfastly professed complete ignorance of any unusual happenings on the night in question, that brought that line of investigation to a sharp halt, unless they could dig up some independent witnesses.

Meredith pulled into the drive of the small detached house that he had recently bought at an extortionate price. Stopping the car in the drive – the garage was still crammed with overflowing furniture and packing cases – he sat for a moment to let his train of thought run its course.

Summers ... he was still comatose in the Royal Infirmary and the doctors refused to forecast when – or even if – he would be fit for questioning. If only he would wake up, he could at least corroborate Iago Price's tale ... every now and then, Meredith had the horrible feeling that the private detective might be a complete nutcase and had invented the whole affair! Though he consoled himself with the fact that Price could hardly have invented that half-burnt lower jaw.

Old Nick climbed wearily out of the car, locked it up and went indoors.

Gwen, his amiable, rotund wife, gave him a smile from in front of the television set, then her hypnotized eyes swung back to the screen. 'It's in the bottom oven, Nick –

mind the plate, it'll be hot.'

As a detective's wife, she had hardly ever managed to put a freshly prepared meal in front of him –he was always late, or never came home at all.

Meredith went through into the kitchen as Gwen called more instructions after him. 'Cake in the cupboard. There are oranges there, too. Should be nice, the man said there was a shipload of the new season's Jaffas just arrived.'

As he sat down to the beautifully cooked, if slightly dried-up supper, he was conscious of a nagging at the back of his mind. For a time he drowned it with other, more immediate thoughts, but as he reached for one of the large oranges, his wife's idle words came back to him.

'… a shipload of new Jaffas' … Jaffa ship … 'gaffer's chips'. He grinned bleakly at his childishness, and impatiently tore the thick skin from the fruit.

But all through the rest of the meal and later, while staring unseeingly at some inane thriller film, the similarity of the phrases kept niggling at his mind.

As there seemed nothing he could do about it, he forced it to the back of his brain. Yet later, when lying in his oversized bed and staring at the ceiling, the words crept back into his consciousness and hovered around until he slipped down the dark slope to sleep.

Next morning, Meredith found that the business of the oranges had incubated in his mind overnight and now refused to be subdued. He was still in his dressing gown when he went downstairs to phone Ellis at home.

In London, he would have made the enquiries himself, in order to limit the circle of people to whom he might make a fool of himself. But he didn't yet know his way around Cardiff sufficiently well to do this and a few words to Bob Ellis would save time, if not his face. Twenty minutes later, the DI rang back.

'Took a long time,' he apologized, 'but Sunday morning is hopeless for tracking people down. Anyway, you seem to have hit something, sir.'

'Well?' barked Meredith, covering his thankfulness with an ungrateful grunt.

'I got on to the Transport Police at the docks, then the harbourmaster's sidekick and finally a shipping company agent.'

Meredith fretted away at Ellis's long-winded approach, but the other man was almost at the meat. 'There's a boat due tonight from Marseilles – half her cargo is Jaffa oranges from Haifa. She's on a regular general cargo run, always brings oranges this time of year, sometimes calls at Genoa and Alexandria as well.' Meredith grunted again and thought hard.

Like almost everything else in the damned case, there could be a perfectly ordinary explanation for what was hardly even a coincidence. Firstly, was 'gaffer's chips' really anything like 'Jaffa ship'? And if so, was the fact significant that such a ship was due on the night mentioned?

And what possible connection could a gang of suspected lorry-hijackers have with an ocean-going vessel ... surely they were not turning their criminal talents to piracy or going into the fruit business!

So many questions – and only one way to get an answer.

'We'll check on this, Ellis – just in case ... what's the name of the ship?'

'The *Akra Siros*, sir ... Greek owned. She's a regular caller here. The agent said she had a mixed crew, mostly Greek but some Frenchmen and Levantines.'

The phone rasped against Meredith's morning stubble as his thoughts took a rapid new turn. The Levant – Alexandria – Genoa – Marseilles. He needed no crystal ball to find a common factor here, which would interest any police officer or Customs man. These were some of the main stations on the drug road from the East, either as halfway houses for opium or cannabis or for the conversion of crude opium into heroin in illegal laboratories, mainly in Turkey and Southern France.

He still couldn't see where this fitted in with Ismail, but it was better to be safe than sorry.

'Ellis, get on to the Drugs Squad and see if they've got any thoughts about this set-up. Better speak to the Customs Waterguard too; they might want to be in on it. We may have to have a reception party for the *Akra Siros*.'

Feeling slightly ashamed at leaving it all to Ellis, he went off for a shave.

High tide was just after midnight, but by eleven o'clock there was sufficient water at the Queen's Dock entrance for the *Akra Siros* to get into the locks.

The fog had cleared and the rain had stopped, but there was a keen wind as the policemen and Customs officers stood on the Pierhead and watched the ship approaching.

There was no real need for Meredith and Ellis to be there, but curiosity had got the better of the chief superintendent, mixed with a need to know if he was making a fool of himself. Bundled into their overcoats, the two CID men stood with Watkins, the detective inspector who dealt with drugs among a ragbag of other duties.

'Never heard any whispers about this ship, sir,' said Watkins in a mildly aggrieved voice. He moved closer and carefully stood so that Old Nick was between him and the wind. 'The number of drug hauls we've had on the docks is damn-all, anyway – most of the stuff comes from London and the south coast.'

'Doesn't mean it doesn't happen,' muttered Meredith, 'only that you haven't caught 'em at it.' The possibility of his pride soon taking a nosedive, if nothing was found, made his mood none the sweeter.

As the black shape of the ship approached behind a tug, the Preventive officer from the Customs and Excise broke away from his waiting Rummage crew and came over to the policemen.

'We'll board her right away, Mr Meredith, and I'll go straight to see the Master – I've got five men for a search. Though, of course, it might take days to go right through the whole ship, if anything is hidden in the holds. But we'll have a quick look through the crew's quarters tonight. Anything more will have to wait until morning.

Old Nick nodded gloomily. As the ship got nearer, it seemed to look more and more like a mountain. The possibility of finding a small package in that great mass of steel seemed an impossibility.

The rush of water from the lock had stopped and the outer gates were slowly opening. They flattened into their recesses in the granite walls and the leading tug entered the dock, straining the towering bows of the ship against the blustery wind.

The *Akra Siros* was an old vessel, an ex-Liberty ship surviving from the war. Though loaded, she rose high in the water and tended to catch the gusting wind. Her bows slid past the gates, then a squall swung her stern around. The rusty plating on her port quarter rubbed along the quayside, raising a shower of sparks and a hideous grinding noise. The stern tug hauled her off and she came to a stop in the lock with no more protests.

As the gates closed, the ship was warped in to the lock side and an ordinary painter's ladder was thrust over the rail for the people who huddled on the quay.

Port Health officials and the ship's agent clambered aboard, then the Preventive officer led his Rummage crew on deck. The senior man went straight to the bridge, while the other Customs men split up and went various ways, their experience telling them the most likely places for a quick check on contraband.

Though the *Akra Siros* was loosely tied up while the lock filled, she was slowly prancing back and forth a few feet in the wind and the long ladder swayed and rocked in spite of its lashings.

The three detectives clambered clumsily aboard and stood awkwardly on the cold deck, now deserted.

'We're a bit off our beat here, sir,' said Ellis, his teeth chattering, 'Let's get up there, where the Customs chap went.'

They groped their way up ladders and by trial and error found their way to the captain's flat below the bridge.

The Preventive officer was talking to the ship's master just inside the open door of his day-cabin. He was a florid, bad-tempered Frenchman and he seemed not to be taking too kindly to the prospect of an extensive search of his vessel.

'How do I know what my crew are up to?' he demanded. 'They change every trip – I do not know the names of half of them!' He waved his hands about angrily and was obviously impatient to get back to drinking with the agent who hovered in the background.

The Customs man winked at Meredith and they all left the captain's quarters to go down to the 'fo'c'sle', which, paradoxically, was right in the stern of the ship.

As they crossed the after-deck, one of the Rummage crew dashed out of a door in the stern quarters and ran to the ship's rail. He leant out over the side and yelled something into the darkness.

The Preventive officer broke into a run and the police followed him. Though there were bulkhead lights and a cargo floodlight in the mainmast rigging, the deck was full of shadows, and Meredith fell sprawling over some unidentifiable piece of metal.

He fell heavily and pulled himself up, cursing fluently.

Bob Ellis doubled back to help him, but the senior man shook him off impatiently. 'I'm all right – what the hell's the panic about?' They joined the two Customs men and Watkins, who stood at the rail, pointing at the dark water.

The ship only occupied two-thirds of the width of the

lock and a stretch of inky-black water lay between them and the opposite quay.

'Someone threw a package through an open porthole down below,' snapped the Rummage crewman. 'Fred Lloyd has got him all right, but I'm trying to see if the packet is still afloat.'

They all searched the water with their eyes, but it was an abyss of blackness down there.

The inner lock gates had just opened and a small rowing boat appeared in the gap, being sculled by a man in the stern. The *Akra Siros* was being put on buoys in the middle of the dock for the night and the boatmen were there to take out the hawsers.

The Customs officer put his hands to his mouth and bellowed down the lock, 'Boatman! Come up the lock – quickly.'

A couple more shouts brought the little skiff nearer and it stopped directly beneath them. By then, other Customs men had got all the deck lights switched on and a wander lamp hung over the side.

The illumination was still feeble, but was enough for the man in the boat to locate what they were looking for. Minutes later, the Preventive officer was holding a brown package the size of a small brick, wrapped in oiled paper inside a polythene bag.

Almost before he had touched it, he said 'Cannabis!'

He smelt it and nodded in satisfaction, then handed it over to Watkins, who did the same.

'Better see the merchant who dumped this, said Meredith grimly, after a cursory look at the packet.

Inside the unattractive crew's quarters, they found another member of the Rummage crew standing guard over a dismal-looking fellow with dark skin and a great hooked nose. He stared at the floor and refused to speak at all.

The ship's First Officer – a Greek – appeared and

reluctantly identified the culprit as a Lebanese deckhand, a regular who had been with the ship for three or four trips in and out of Cardiff.

'And I'll bet he handed over a brick-sized packet every time,' muttered Meredith to the discomfited Drug Squad inspector.

Nothing would induce the man to speak, though the Mate said that he understood English well enough. The Customs man who had run up on deck said that he had caught the Lebanese throwing something through the porthole just as he came into the mess room. It was impossible to say where it had been hidden, but there were a dozen places big enough to conceal it – all the seats around the tables were boxes with padded tops and would have held half a ton of hashish.

'Better give this place the old toothcomb treatment,' said the senior Customs officer, 'but I've a feeling we've had all our luck for tonight.'

'It was luck enough that the stuff floated instead of going to the bottom,' said Ellis thankfully.

Watkins looked at the package in his hand. 'It's raw stuff – much lighter than the purified resin. That would have gone down like a stone. This waxed paper and the air trapped inside the plastic bag kept it up.'

Meredith murmured in Ellis's ear. 'We've got to try and break this deckhand down and tie him in with Ismail, or we've wasted a whole night as far as that side of things is concerned. Let's get him back to Bute Street.'

Twenty minutes later, after some mugs of nightshift tea, they sat down in the CID room of the Docks station and tried to wring something from the blank-faced Levantine.

After a quarter of an hour, all they had achieved was ten repetitions of the word 'Consul'. Meredith's eyes were starting to get bloodshot and he had to restrain himself from flinging furniture at the infuriatingly uncooperative sailor.

At last, throwing the Judges' Rules to the winds, he stooped menacingly over the seated deckhand and brought his clenched fist gently up under his nose. 'Listen, sailor-boy,' he hissed, 'you get this – chop-chop! ... you don't tell me anything, then you go to jail so long your mother and father will forget you ever lived – savvy?'

This had an immediate effect. Meredith's pent-up passion, more than the actual words, caused the man to suddenly remember his English.

'I don't know nothing, boss,' he muttered sullenly.

'Who were you to give the packet to, eh?' snapped Old Nick.

There was no answer and the chief superintendent suddenly slammed his other hand on to back of the chair. An innocent move, but it did the trick. The sailor's eyes flicked across and he licked his lips. 'Honest, I don't know. I was to keep it till somebody came to fetch it on ship.'

'What happened the other times – who fetched it then?'

But the magic had gone. Over and over, the Lebanese denied he had ever brought hemp into the country and nothing Meredith or Ellis could pretend to threaten would alter his story.

After an hour they gave up and at two thirty in the morning – and in a very bad temper – Meredith threw himself into his half of the conjugal bed.

His wife stirred slightly. 'Have a nice time, dear?' she murmured and went back to sleep again.

Chapter Nine

Iago Price had spent a miserable weekend.

His self-reproach about Terry Rourke's death had not faded with the passing of the days – rather it had grown stronger in his mind. He had moped about his flat all weekend. His parents were still abroad and the loss of his usual Sunday duty visit to them had thrown him even more upon his own dismal company.

It poured with rain each day and Iago felt that if ever he were to do away with himself, this was the sort of weekend it would happen. At lunchtime, he sat in his frayed dressing gown pecking at a reheated frozen meal and staring glumly at the fungus that was starting to grow on the inside of his window frame.

As he listlessly prodded his 'Tastee-Peez' he wished that Dilys was here. She was not scintillating company, but she was a woman. Iago had never managed to manoeuvre her into his seedy flat – in fact, he had never managed to manoeuvre her anywhere, apart from the Glendower Arms.

He couldn't explain why he was so fascinated by her. She was conceited, as hard as nails, not very intelligent and treated him with about as much affection as her typewriter. Yet he had come to wait eagerly for every working day, so that he could share the same office with her; every evening, the few minutes in the pub was like an assignation with a fairy princess to him.

He had once read some cynic's words who said that a man will eventually fall in love with the most repulsive woman on earth, if she is the only one available. He hardly rated his office as a desert island, but if he had thought about it, the fact of being thrown together for so many hours a day was leading to an inevitable infatuation.

The urge to hug her, kiss and slap her bottom playfully was always with him now – only her cold glare kept him at bay.

She was common, ill-mannered and spoke abominably, but he was rapidly becoming crazed with her. As the rain dribbled down his window panes, fantasies of an alluring Dilys came thick and fast upon poor Iago.

Then he sighed and pushed his plate away – Terry's ghost had returned to drive away Dilys' mirage.

Poor Terry – he had only met the boy for a few minutes, but the feeling of guilt would be with Iago for life unless he found some means of exorcising it.

Tiger Ismail and his crowd had killed Rourke – Iago was convinced of that. Yet it looked as though they were going to get clean away with it. He had had an unofficial word with Ellis on the phone that morning – he was by far the most approachable of the policemen. Ellis had more or less said that there was no evidence at all to connect the restaurant owner with the crime and unless they could unearth some independent witness there was no chance of a charge being brought against Tiger or his cronies.

A little spark of anger began to glow deep in Iago's soul. Just as it had after the car attack, so now a slow burn of determination to do something began to grip him.

The new feeling was infinitely preferable to dull reproach. The sudden excitement it brought made him get up and pace the room, like some latter-day Sherlock Holmes in his long brown dressing gown.

But what was to be done? No more hired assistants. Even if he could find one, he wanted to act himself this time. Not being a Batman or a Simon Templar, he had no talent for bursting in on Tiger and twisting his neck until he confessed.

Iago shambled up and down, his thin stooped figure

searching restlessly for some positive action.

Suddenly he stopped opposite his stereo record player and stared at it. The maker's original design had been deformed by extra wires and connections to a radio, on top of which was a microphone.

Amongst Iago's pitifully few talents was a knack with radio and electrical equipment. He had no theoretical knowledge at all, but a happy ability to join the right wires together to make things work.

He looked now at his mess of apparatus and began thoughtfully to scratch his nose.

He had wanted Terry Rourke to listen for incriminating words in the Cairo Restaurant –a wild hope considering that the lad could hardly have listened at Tiger's keyhole for twenty-four hours of the day. But a microphone could listen for those twenty-four hours, as long as it was strategically placed and had someone or something to keep a vigil at the other end of the wire.

Iago dropped to his knees and began toying with the plastic leads and the microphone itself. If only he could plant it in the right place … he came to an abrupt stop. He had been in there once himself and Terry had been caught at the same game. Ridiculous to think of gate-crashing or infiltrating there again.

It took his pedestrian mind some minutes of frowning thought to arrive at an alternative scheme. He impulsively tore off his dressing gown, clambered into sweater and slacks and went for his car.

He made a quick circuit through the deserted, rain-soaked city centre and then went on to the docks. Then he returned home, having seen all he wanted in one quick drive-past of the Cairo Restaurant. Back in the flat, he set to work feverishly on his equipment, struggling with coils of thin wire, screwdriver, headphones and a small battery tape recorder, which he had borrowed from Lewis Evans weeks before.

Launched on this new flight of his butterfly mind, the hours flew by in almost ecstatic happiness; he almost forgot the grim reason for all his activity as he wrestled with leads and soldering iron.

When there was nothing left to do, he went down to whisper his secret plan across the bar of the Glendower Arms. The landlord's only comment was, 'Make sure the police send back my tape recorder when they lock you up in a safe place, Iago.'

Next morning, he had to explain it all again to Dilys. She was incredulous, scathing and contemptuous by turns, but, to his annoyance, not once did she mention the risk to himself.

'I'll have to look after this flaming office by myself again, then,' was her final comment.

He sulked at her, 'Nothing to do – just hold the fort. Take any jobs that come in, but explain there may be a delay of a day or two due to pressure of business.'

She sneered back at him, 'Pressure of business my eye! … if it wasn't for two divorces and that credit thing, you could spend all your time playing with bits of wire – apart from the little detail of paying my wages and the rent.'

Her darkened eyelids flickered dangerously as she stabbed him in the chest with a red talon. 'When are you going to grow up, Iago?' she demanded.

His sagging moustache came erect with indignation.

'Look, Dill … that young chap Rourke, he got himself killed doing my dirty work. I may be weak in the head, but I'm damned if that lot in Bute Street are going to get off scot-free. This idea may be a dead loss, but at least I'll have tried – and that means a hell of a lot to me!'

There was a ring of sincerity in his voice that got through even Dilys' thick skin and she backed down.

'OK, have it your own way,' she sighed, 'but watch what you're doing … you know you're not safe to be let out alone.'

This was the nearest she ever got to expressing concern for him, but Iago was strangely contented with it. He went back into his half of the office for a final fiddle with the contents of the battered suitcase that held all his equipment. He had yards of different coloured flex, joined by clumsy insulating tape joints. There was a small transistorized amplifier scrounged months ago from his sister's baby alarm. Lewis's small Japanese recorder shared the rest of the case with a pair of ex-army headphones. He checked all the items for the tenth time and snapped the case shut.

'I'll be back in an hour,' he said, as he went through to the outer door. 'Tell you what, I'll treat you to a fried rice at the Ming Hong – might be the last square meal I get until tomorrow.'

She sniffed and muttered something he hoped was agreement.

Leaving the case in his car, he walked into town and made for the offices of an estate agent whose name he had read on a sign in Tiger Bay the day before. This was a small, obscure firm who specialized in seedy business properties. As he climbed the gloomy stairs to their den, he reflected that their standard of office accommodation was only a shade above his own.

A few minutes' tapping on a grimy glass door eventually brought an adenoidal girl. She seemed faintly surprised that anyone should want to enquire about a property, but at length unearthed a creased paper giving details of a shop in Bute Street.

'Dis d' one?' she murmured through her blocked sinuses.

Iago glanced at it and nodded. 'Can I have the key, please?'

She looked at him suspiciously. Asking about a property was bad enough, but actually waiting to see it!

She grumbled to herself and vanished for another five minutes into the dusty recesses of the office. Returning with a Yale key on a grubby luggage label, she slapped it on the counter. 'Mr Lloyd says he supposes it's all right – nobody to go with you, mind. Sign here.' He signed and made his escape.

He went nowhere near Bute Street, but only to the nearest Woolworth's, where he got a copy of the key cut in a few minutes. After a decent interval, padded out by a pint of beer in the Buccaneer bar, he took the original key back and told the uninterested girl that he was sorry but it wasn't the sort of place for which he was looking.

He gave Dilys the promised lunch at a Chinese restaurant, his spirits mounting with every minute. The girl by no means shared them.

'And just how long do you reckon you'll be off on this damn fool nonsense?' she demanded.

'You're nagging me, Dill – just like a wife,' he said happily.

She glared at him. 'That's about as much action as you'll ever get in the wife direction, so get any nasty ideas out of your head right now,' she snapped. 'I asked how long you'll be out of the office.'

'All week if needs be,' he said airily. 'I'm taking a Thermos and a couple of bottles, as well as some food. I'll stay there until the early hours, then knock off until next morning.'

'Or die of old age!' she retorted sarcastically.

But nothing could dampen his enthusiasm for his latest brainstorm. As soon as the girl had gone back to mope by the office phone, Iago drove down to the remnants of Tiger Bay. He parked the dented old Jaguar on one of the plentiful patches of bare ground, well away from the vicinity of the cafe.

Before leaving the car, he struggled into a set of faded dungarees, added a cloth cap and a plastic mackintosh, then perched a pair of glasses on his nose.

Clutching his battered suitcase under his arm, he walked off towards Bute Street, fondly imagining himself to be the image of a typical employee of the South Wales Electricity Board.

He circuited the restaurant by the back lanes so that he could approach the next door premises from the other direction.

His new key worked smoothly in the lock and, more by luck than the impenetrability of his disguise, he got inside without being seen.

Iago closed the door with a sigh of relief and leant against the inside for a moment while the inner tensions faded away. Then he stripped off the cap, raincoat and spectacles and lugged his case up the stairs to the second floor of the deserted building.

Here came his first setback.

He found the trapdoor to the loft easily enough – about twelve feet up, directly over the upper landing! Iago groaned and began a search of the rooms.

He scoured hopefully through each floor and even in the yard and outhouses at the back, but there was no stepladder.

The whole place was thick with dirt, dust and fallen plaster, but very little else. He made an inventory of any object that could be climbed upon and started dragging what there was towards the landing. To be baulked at the post by such a stupid detail as reaching the trapdoor was infuriating, though typical of Iago's mad impulses.

After half an hour, sheer trial and error won the day. The upper rooms had a few mouldering bits of furniture lying around, stuff that had not been worth taking away. Two small tables, a chair and a cupboard, dragged painfully from different rooms, made a tottering heap below the trap. After two collapses, Iago managed to scramble through the hatchway and drag his case up on a length of strong string.

The filth in the loft was appalling.

By the light of his large rubber-covered torch, he looked around from the edge of the hole. At first sight, he seemed to be in a jungle of grey vines and creepers. They were dust-covered cobwebs hanging in festoons from the rafters. It seemed unlikely that the place had been entered since the building was put up, some eighty years before.

Nerving himself to endure the filthy embraces of the foliage, Iago tripped delicately from joist to joist in the direction of the Cairo Restaurant.

The cobwebs formed an almost opaque screen, but after a few steps he breathed a cautious sigh of relief – there was no wall between the loft of this empty shop and next door. If there had been, the fiasco over the trapdoor would have been eclipsed by total defeat. In all fairness, he had thought of this possibility. In fact, the object of his short trip on the previous day had been partly to confirm his hunch. As well as making sure that there was an empty shop next to Tiger's place and to get the name of the estate agent, he wanted to check that the arrangements of doors and windows of the adjacent premises suggested that they had once been a single large building, in which case the attics would almost certainly be continuous. Now he had proved his point – the beam of the torch struggled through the murk and failed to hit any wall after he had crossed a dozen or so joists.

A little further on, he found the boundary line with next door.

There were cross baulks of timber of a different vintage marking the partition wall, and major alterations of the electric wiring separating the supply to the two premises. Obviously, his guess about the age of all the cobwebs must have been wrong, but the alterations were still quite ancient.

The sight of the 'frontier' made him appreciate the

nearness of the enemy and he tiptoed back to the hatch and sat on its edge. As he took all his electrical stuff from the case, he tried to recall the sketchy description that poor Terry Rourke had given him of the upper floor of the Cairo Restaurant ... a large lounge across the front and a bedroom next to the landing. So he should be able to locate the centre of the lounge by the lighting wires going to the ceiling rose and the switch cables should mark the line of the wall.

Having no real plan in mind beyond this point, Iago was sublimely unworried about his next moves. The success of getting so far, seemed an omen for inevitable success.

He coupled up the last wires of his Heath Robinson apparatus – more like a bad dream from an Emmett cartoon – and rested the tape recorder on the lip of the hatch.

Carefully, he went back across the joists, paying out the thin flex behind him. Reaching the line of the partition wall, he hesitated. It was mid-afternoon and he had no idea if Ismail or any of his cronies were likely to be in the room below.

He listened intently, but apart from the muffled sounds of traffic in Bute Street, he could hear nothing.

His heart thumping, he worked his way cat-footed into enemy territory, crouching under the rafters to try and avoid the creaky areas of the centre of the loft. The joists were made of timber that shamed the skimpiness of modern builders, but even so they gave an occasional squeak that brought Iago's stomach up into his neck.

He traced the electric wires to the light socket – they were so encrusted by dirt that only a slight humping of the general grime gave away their position.

As he worked towards the centre, the creaking of the beams got worse, but in a few steps he was there and had placed the microphone face down on the lath and plaster.

Next to it he put the baby alarm amplifier. He had no idea whether or not it would pick up speech from below, but he just had to wait and see, using his inexhaustible optimism. On tiptoe, he went back across the foetid loft and sat with his legs dangling through the trapdoor.

He slipped on the earphones, plugged into the monitor socket on the tape recorder and settled down to wait for something to happen.

During the late afternoon, while Iago Price was dozing among the cobwebs, Tiger Ismail and three of his colleagues were having an earnest talk with the police.

Detective Sergeant Rees arrived at the Cairo Restaurant about four o'clock with the firm request to see Mr Ismail and escort him to the police station 'to assist the police in their inquiries'.

Tiger was fast asleep in his bedroom – Uncle Ahmed roused him and brought him downstairs without Iago getting so much as a whisper in his headphones.

Dai Rees was polite but determined. Tiger thought of standing on his legal rights and refusing to say anything or go anywhere unless he was charged. But on reflection, he guessed that he might come off better if he avoided antagonizing the police more than necessary. He accepted a lift in the police car standing outside and in two minutes was going through the doors of the police station.

Tiger was slightly disturbed to see Nikos Kalvos and Archie Vaughan sitting on hard chairs in the corridor with a large, impassive policeman planted between them.

On his way to the CID room he caught the sound of Joe Davies' voice coming from an adjacent interview room. His annoyance deepened, though it was still far from being apprehension.

The sergeant led him into the small, back room, where the beetle-browed face of Nicholas Meredith scowled at him across a desk.

No one asked him to sit down – there was no chair in

any case. Dai Rees slid on to a table behind him and ostentatiously took out his notebook.

'The time has come for a good talk, Ismail,' grated Meredith.

Tiger said nothing. He knew the form and was confident that nothing was going to happen.

Meredith knew that he knew and was aggravated before he even started.

'Where were you between eight o'clock and midnight last night?' he demanded.

'I don't have to tell you, do I?' said the olive-skinned young man easily. There was no insolence in his voice, just a rather bored statement of fact.

Meredith held himself in check with an effort. 'You'll have to tell me sooner or later – and if it's later, the fact won't escape notice. Now come on – stop arsing about!'

Ismail smiled humourlessly. 'Are you going to arrest me – and if so, what for?'

Meredith felt his blood pressure climb a notch or two. 'You know damned well I'm not arresting you – not just at this moment, anyway. Whether I do in the future depends on what you tell me now.'

Tiger remained silent.

'Where were you last night – and what have you got to say again about your movements last Wednesday night?'

Tiger sighed – a loud, over-dramatic sigh. 'Last night, I was in the cafe until ten ... give you a dozen witnesses, if you like. Then I drove to the Roma Club and stayed there till two ... ditto another dozen witnesses. Next question?'

Old Nick, stopped dead on that one as he had expected, abruptly switched to another tack.

'Ever been in the basement of the Compass Building in Tydfil Street?'

Ismail's smoothly arched eyebrows rose. 'Yes – when I was a kid. My great-uncle works there. We been through all this, mister!'

Meredith ignored him. 'You swear you've not been in there this last week?'

Ismail looked elaborately around him. 'Swear? We in the witness box already!'

Dai Rees looked at Meredith, half expecting to see smoke wreathing from his nostrils. 'Don't act too smart, Tiger,' he muttered from behind.

Meredith glared at the sergeant, who subsided into his notebook.

'Any of your numerous family work the boats at present?' he snapped.

'At a quick guess – about ten. Why?'

'Ever heard of a ship called the *Akra Siros*?'

Tiger, having heard that morning of the seizure of his cannabis consignment, was ready for this one. 'No – none of our family on that one.'

'Do you know that a ship of that name arrived in Cardiff last night?'

Tiger was beginning to enjoy himself with this thick copper and, over-confident, put his foot right in it. 'How would I know – I run a restaurant, not a wholesale fruiterer's! ' As the words left his mouth, he cursed himself. It was not even a trap – he had thrown that one away for nothing.

Meredith's saturnine face actually smiled. A slow burner that left Tiger well out of the joke.

'Wholesale fruit? What *can* you mean?' he repeated sarcastically. His face snapped back into a stony mask. 'Come on, you've dropped yourself in it now,' he said briskly. He stood up and stood a full head above the younger man. 'I happen to know that you knew all about that ship's arrival –and you just confirmed it for me … so cough, Ismail –let's have it all.'

He dragged his chair right around the desk with a sweep of his long arm and planted it behind Tiger. 'Sit down – there's a pen and paper on the desk. You can write it yourself or Sergeant Rees will take it at your dictation.'

But Tiger was a tougher nut than that … he had recovered completely from his *faux pas*.

'I don't know what you're talking about,' he said woodenly.

Meredith spent the next ten minutes going through chapter and verse of the cannabis incident, accusing Ismail at the end of each sentence. But Tiger was unmoved. Though he realized that he had compromised himself badly by that silly slip of the tongue, he also knew that as evidence, it was next to useless.

Meredith knew it too; where the blustering, steamroller technique might have succeeded in forcing a lesser crook into a confession, it failed hopelessly with Ismail, who was in a different class. Tiger knew that unless one of the other three let something drop, he was safe enough, though the hot breath of the law was getting uncomfortably near his neck.

When Meredith finally ran out of steam, he tried one last gambit. 'Right – are you going to give me a statement or am I going to charge you? Conspiracy, Dangerous Drugs Act, umpteen Customs and Excise Acts – the lot.'

Tiger was unimpressed. 'I'll write you a statement telling you where I was at the times you mention,' he said easily. 'Apart from that, I refuse to say any more without my solicitor being here … and as I know damn well you haven't the slightest intention of slapping a charge on me, I'll be off home.'

Meredith sighed, but he was satisfied with his progress. At least both of them knew where they stood now. Meredith knew that Ismail was involved and Ismail knew that the police had nothing concrete to hang on him.

There was no offer of a lift back to the cafe. Tiger found that Joe Davies and the Greek had already left, but Archie was hanging around the front door when he went out.

They set off to walk the length of Bute Street together. The little man started to jabber about his recent interview, but Tiger stopped him. 'Save it until we get back – we got big talking to do.'

A few minutes later they were all seated in the upstairs lounge with a drink apiece.

Tiger took the stage and went to the centre of the room to stand directly under Iago's microphone.

Tiger's dark eyes swept around the other three. He was worried, but his unflappable mind was computing the odds, as it did every night at the gaming tables.

'We're right up against it, boys,' he began in a crisp voice. 'No good cribbing about what's done, but I hope you'll remember that it was you that dropped us into this trouble, not me. Still, we got to look ahead, not back.'

Up in the loft next door his voice suddenly brought Iago Price back to life. After several hours of alternate dozing and cursing the cramp in his legs, he had eaten all his sandwiches and emptied his Thermos. He had watched the hands of his luminous watch creep around with increasing despair, as nothing at all had happened.

The sudden buzz of a voice in his headphones galvanized him into awareness. He reached for the 'Record' button on the recorder, but then realized that all he was hearing was an indistinguishable buzz that was undoubtedly a human voice, but no more.

As he fiddled desperately with the contacts on his tape machine, Tiger Ismail got on to the constructive part of his speech.

'We've been rumbled over the smuggling – I don't know how … even you lot wouldn't be so dumb as to shoot your mouths off about that, but somehow the fuzz got the news from somewhere.'

Joe Davies scowled. He didn't take kindly to personal criticism – he was a frustrated leader, not a yes-man like Nikos and Archie.

Tiger ignored him. 'The coppers can't pin anything on us yet – probably never will, but they got a pretty good idea we're mixed up in it and they'll have their noses on our trail like a pack of bloodhounds from now on.'

'What's all this leading to, Tiger?' grunted Davies.

Ismail smiled mirthlessly at him. 'It means we're all washed up, Joe – that what it means.'

They stared at him owlishly as he enlarged on, the decision.

'Tonight we split up – for good. I've had a bellyful of being let down by you lot. But we pull one last job for old time's sake – then we evaporate!'

The other three shuffled in their seats with restless excitement.

'You mean the Stores?' squeaked Archie Vaughan. His voice was more high-pitched than the others and by some trick of acoustics, his words came over loud and clear in Iago's headphones.

Without knowing their context, they meant nothing to him, but served to heighten his mounting frustration at the failure of his apparatus.

'Yeah – the Stores!' confirmed Tiger easily. 'I had a word with Betty on the phone lunchtime ... she says that though a Monday is usually a poor day for takings, the Christmas Club has just paid out. They're having a bumper run and there should be a couple of thousand in the kitty by tonight.'

'They'll dump it all in the night safe,' objected Joe Davies, almost glad to be able to pick a hole in the boss's plans.

Ismail shook his head. 'They do that on Tuesdays, Thursdays, Fridays and Saturdays, says Betty. She's been casing the place for a week. They don't normally take enough on Mondays and Wednesdays to make it worthwhile ... tonight will be different with the Christmas shopping spree just starting, but habit dies hard. Unless she rings up by six o'clock and says they've dumped the loot in the bank, we move in at ten o'clock.'

'How's she going to know – she's only been working on the counter for a week?' objected Joe.

'Her pal in the accounts office – she got in tow with her even while she was hooking Summers at the Bank … the girl got her the job at David Powell's … Betty's conned her right up to the hilt.' While they were putting their heads together over the details of their break-in at the big store, Iago Price was going almost berserk over their heads. He had caught the odd word here and there, but not sufficient to get any real idea of what they were talking about – only enough to whet his appetite to breaking point!

He checked and rechecked his end of the circuit and could find no fault with it. He was forced to the conclusion that the microphone was just too weak to pick up voices through the plaster of the ceiling.

Without any clear idea of what he could do, he started to work his way across the joists towards the offending microphone. He thought vaguely that if he could move it around a little, he might find a thinner area of ceiling which would transmit more sound. He kept his headphones on, trailing the wire behind him as he tiptoed across the dividing line of old timber.

Down below, the plotters were back on more worrying problems.

'What happens when we get this stuff tonight?' grunted Nikos Kalvos.

'Split five ways, each throw a bit in the kitty for Uncle Ahmed and Florrie – then you're on your own.'

Joe Davies scratched his ear pensively. 'This is the end, then?'

Tiger stared at him coolly. 'You've had it good for a couple of years – what you've all done with your share of the pickings is your concern, but if you'd had any sense and salted most of it away, you'll be all set up. If you've blown the lot on booze and women, then hard luck!'

The looks on their faces showed plainly that none of the others had put any away for a rainy day such as this one. Tiger sniffed disdainfully. 'If you're all broke, there'll be at least a few hundred apiece coming tonight – and maybe some small stuff like jewellery if we're lucky.'

Archie Vaughan seemed near to tears. 'We'll have all the coppers in Wales breathing down our neck if we pull a big job like this! How do we know they ain't got a tail on us all the time, anyway?'

Joe looked at him contemptuously. 'They have, mate … there's a chap on the corner been reading the same page of the same *Echo* this last two hours – he arrived just as we went up the nick, so Ahmed says. But we can slip twits like that with our ankles tied together.'

Archie was still broken-hearted. 'Where'm I gonna go afterwards?' he squeaked.

'Hitch a lift towards London or the Midlands.' suggested Tiger with evident disinterest.

Joe looked at the smooth Middle Eastern face with curiosity. 'What about you, Tiger – where you holing up, eh?'

Ismail gave him a stony look. 'The less you know, the less you can grass, Joe … in case anyone's forgotten, the *Akra Siros* is sailing tomorrow night, back to Antwerp and the Mediterranean – not that I'm thinking of getting a lift, but you might be interested, Nikos.'

The Greek nodded glumly. He was a wanted man in both Athens and Cyprus, so the prospect didn't excite him greatly.

Tiger had, in fact, got his escape route well organized. Typically, he had looked ahead to this sort of crisis long before, and had planned to drive to Bristol – in a hired car, not his own – then a night flight to the Continent, where he had managed to accumulate a minor fortune smuggled out in sterling on numerous holiday trips and converted to

Swiss francs on the other side.

'How close are the rozzers on us, Tiger?' asked Joe. 'They were pretty nasty this afternoon, though they didn't seem to have much in the way of evidence to throw at us?'

'They're bluffing at the moment, but they're watching like hawks for one of us to put a foot wrong over either the Rourke business, Summers or that packet of hemp … and knowing you bloody lot, one of you is sure to come unstuck sooner or later. That's why we're fading out after tonight's job. The fuzz won't expect us to pull a job like this while they're still screwing us over the others. That's why it's going to go off OK'

He began his pacing up and down, the tensions inside him giving the lie to his inscrutable face. 'One slip and we're blown right open – we can't risk it. Even if you twits keep your mouths shut, there's always the chance the coppers will turn up someone from outside. Uncle Arif is safe enough, but if they dig up somebody who saw you going down that basement – or find some fingerprint or bit of scientific whizz, we'll be up the creek pretty sharp!'

Upstairs, a nearly demented Iago was holding his breath as he trod on a groaning beam while he stooped to move the microphone. A few tantalizing words had got through, but he was still only getting a twentieth part of what was being said down below.

As he moved the instrument, the friction against the plaster was like thunder in the headphones. He slid the microphone over the small hole where the wires went down to the light socket and suddenly Archie Vaughan's voice came through quite clearly.

'How do we know that everything is going to work out tonight –is Betty all lined up?'

Tiger's reply was muffled, but still audible. 'If the cash stays on the premises, so will she. She's going to hide away somewhere and spring the side door for us at ten o'clock.'

The deep voice of the Greek came through next. 'I hope that I have not lost my touch, Tiger – it's years since I petered a safe.'

'You've still got some of that "jelly", haven't you?' said Ismail sharply. 'If you can't coax it, blow it! We're not going to be fussy tonight.'

Iago quivered with excitement. He had left the recorder running and this should be on the tape now. He was in a quandary … by the sound of what had just been said, he had little time to get back and convince the police before the balloon went up … but should he wait and try to get something more damning in respect of Terry Rourke or Summers?

His impulsive nature won easily and he decided to cut and run with what he had already.

His heart bounded with excitement as he turned to begin making his way from joist to joist in the direction of the empty shop. He forgot he was still trailing the microphone lead behind him. As he lifted a foot and moved it towards the next timber, the flex wrapped itself around his ankle and brought him down.

With a muffled yell he fell forwards and his right leg plunged through the brittle plaster to dangle horribly below the ceiling of the lounge.

Chapter Ten

Nicholas Meredith leant his angular body against the edge of Bob Ellis's desk. He wore his usual black outfit and his hat was already on' his head. His car keys dangled from his bony fingers, as he was just about to set off for home.

'We started to crack 'em this afternoon, Ellis,' he said in a low, harsh voice.

The detective inspector nodded. 'Dai Rees told me about that slip of Tiger's over the fruit boat – but apparently he shut up like a clam afterwards.'

Old Nick nodded. 'But we know where we are now – he's a villain, all right! They'll slip up again before long. If we can get just one solid bit of evidence against them … just one – we'll have 'em!'

Ellis looked doubtful. 'You won't get a slip from Tiger again – not him, sir! If anyone coughs, it'll be Archie or the Greek. Not Ismail or Davies, they're tough nuts, they are.'

'I don't give a damn who it is,' snapped Meredith. 'We're on the winning side now, the only place they can go is down! Just one bit of real evidence, that's all I ask.'

For a moment, Bob Ellis thought his superior was going to go on his knees in the CID room and start praying for the fingerprint men or the laboratory staff to materialize some incriminating proof out of thin air.

But Old Nick's next question surprised him.

'You know them better than me, Ellis – d'you think they'll run?'

The other man rubbed his nose thoughtfully. 'Hard to say, sir – we don't know how hard-pressed they are, do we? I don't think they will, really. After all, we've got enough on them even to manufacture a holding charge. The only pressure might be psychological – they don't know what we know about any other jobs they've done.'

This tortuous logic was not much help and Meredith levered himself off the desk and glanced up at the clock.

'Half past six … an early night tonight. My missus will wonder what's wrong if I go home now!'

Ellis had noticed that his boss had become more talkative today – normally, he could go half a week without saying a word beyond what was absolutely necessary for the running of the department. He wondered if it was a good sign or a bad one … slowly, the two men were getting to know each other, feeling their way into each other's characters like a pair of newlyweds. Though Charlie Harris was officially the second-in-command, he was an insensitive red tape merchant and it was Bob Ellis who seemed closest to Meredith.

'Well, see you in the morning,' said Old Nick unwisely and loped away to his car.

Ellis stayed behind to bang away at his typewriter at some monthly crime figures, his mind half on the papers and half on the problem sitting down in Tiger Bay.

The forensic laboratory had come up with some fancy chemical tests that proved definitely that the ashes in which the jaw was found came from the furnace of the Compass Building … but as they already knew this by a process of exclusion, it didn't take them very much further forward.

The old caretaker had been grilled again, without an atom of progress being made. The daytime boilerman had been seen and knew nothing at all of any unusual goings-on.

Every house in the surrounding streets had been visited and the occupants questioned about any mysterious visits to the office block at night, but again no one knew anything – or if they did, they were keeping it to themselves. Detectives went through the local public houses and shops and questioned the regulars in the same vein, but all they got were black looks and surly answers.

The pathologist and dentists had done all manner of fancy tests and measurements – including X-rays – on the long-suffering jawbone. The medical people seemed to get great academic delight in this messing about and declared once again that the deceased was none other than Terence Rourke. But as this was no longer in the slightest doubt, it got the investigators no further forward.

The affair of the *Akra Siros* was more hopeful, at first sight. It pleased the Customs men and was a blow against the drug trade in South Wales, though Ellis agreed with the Excise men that the cannabis was probably destined for London or the English Midlands, rather than for local consumption.

As far as using the ship incident to nail Tiger and his boys, it fell far short of success.

The fact that they had got on to the smuggling at all was little more than an inspired guess by Meredith. Until Tiger's slip that afternoon about the fruit boat, Ellis had only been half-convinced that the whole thing wasn't a coincidence. In any case, the evidential value in a court was almost nil.

He sighed and bent to his typewriter again. The Docks case was a welcome diversion, but it seemed to have run out of steam at the moment – and now the rest of the city crime had to be dealt with, as usual. Cars were still stolen, dud cheques passed and shops broken into – and probably always would be, he thought glumly, looking at the pile of reports lying heavily in his desk tray.

The appearance of Iago's leg through the ceiling shocked even the tough men below into a stunned silence.

As the worn elastic-sided shoe dangled above his head,

Archie Vaughan managed a strangled 'God Almighty!' but Tiger came back to life in a more practical way. He leapt onto a small coffee table and grabbed the wriggling ankle, which was showing signs of being withdrawn.

'Joe ... Nikos ... get up the flaming loft! Quick! There's a stepladder in the bog ... get going, damn you!'

The two big men lumbered off, leaving Ismail to pinion the leg from below. Even if he had not been clinging to it, it was doubtful whether Iago could have got it free, as the splintered laths were acting like a trap ... the more he pulled, the more the shattered wood dug into his leg.

He had dropped the torch and was crouching on the floor, one foot doubled under him, still supported by a joist. He found himself weakly yelling, 'Let go!' to the abysmal darkness. Scared and in acute discomfort, he was too confused to look ahead to his possible fate ... all he wanted to do was to get his leg free. He still wore the headphones – now dead since the wire snapped –

and these acted as earmuffs, preventing him hearing the scraping of the hatch as Joe levered it open after years of disuse.

Down below, Archie stared fearfully at the disembodied leg. 'Is it the cops?' he whispered to Tiger.

The young Arab was pale, but stony-faced. Things were going from bad to worse, but he kept an iron grip on himself.

'Doesn't matter if it is or not ... we've got to keep him on ice until tonight's job is done.' He raised his voice. 'Joe, you up there yet?'

There was no reply, but a heavy bang as the hatch fell open answered his question.

Changing his grip on the leg, he snapped an order at Vaughan.

'Get down to the front door and keep an eye on the next shop ... he must have got in through there ... tell Uncle Ahmed to watch the back, there might be somebody else trying to slip out. We must know if we've been rumbled … get a move on, man!'

As Archie pattered away, heavy footsteps and muffled voices sounded overhead. The leg began wriggling violently.

'Let him go, Tiger,' came Joe's distant shout. Ismail released the ankle and it was jerked violently upwards, bits of lath snapping off and a snowstorm of plaster flakes billowing down. The shoe stuck at ceiling level and fell off, but the leg vanished through a ragged hole.

'Who was it, Joe?' yelled Tiger through the cavity.

The answer was immediate – and reassuring. 'Not the rozzers … it's that bloody feller – the private eye.'

The clumping reversed across the ceiling and in a moment a dishevelled and dirty Iago was thrust roughly into the room.

Joseph Stalin had him in a painful grip, his arm twisted up behind his back. The Greek came close behind, clutching a tangle of wire and a tape recorder.

'A flaming spy, Tiger – another of 'em,' snarled Joe viciously.

Ismail threw him a venomous look and he dried up immediately, aware of letting yet another bit of evidence fall gratuitously.

'At least it's not the law,' murmured Ismail, his dark eyes staring at the petrified Iago.

'What the hell are we going to do with him?' demanded Joe Davies.

'He had all this stuff up there,' muttered Nikos Kalvos. 'D'you want to hear what's on the tape?'

Tiger waved him away. 'I don't care, as long as it gets lost. Flush it down the loo – or burn it in the kitchen.'

The Greek vanished and Tiger motioned to Joe to put Iago in a chair.

The long-haired lieutenant shoved the enquiry agent roughly into a seat and stood behind him. 'Any messing about and you'll get done!' he growled menacingly.

Iago found his voice at last. Shivering with a mixture of emotion and fright, he made a miserable attempt at bluster.

'You must be mad … the police know I'm here. They'll be coming to look for me if I don't get back by six o'clock.'

Tiger stared at him without a flicker of expression. 'Shut up … you and your interfering have been the cause of all our troubles. You're the one that sent Rourke here snooping.'

'And you killed him … go on then, finish me off as well!' blabbered Iago, in a pathetic bout of bravado.

'Don't know what you're talking about – he walked out of here, we never saw him again, did we, Joe?' Tiger had an eye to the future. Tonight should go well, but if they slipped up and were caught, the last thing he wanted was Iago's corroboration of the strong police suspicions. Joe had already put one of his big feet in it; that was bad enough.

'What did you hear up there?' snapped Tiger, changing the subject.

Iago made a futile attempt to play them at their own game.

'Nothing – couldn't hear a thing. That's how I came to fall through, trying to alter the mike.'

The Arab shrugged indifferently. 'All the same to me.'

Iago's eyes opened like pale blue saucers. His pasty face looked like uncooked bread, with a bacon-rind moustache hung at the centre. 'What you going to do … look, stop this fooling, you've got to let me go. You're all finished now, you know that.'

Tiger stared at him and for an awful moment Iago thought that he was going to give Joe orders to take him out and 'dispose' of him in true Chicago style. The memory of Terry Rourke came flooding back again in horrific detail and the fright almost stopped his vital functions – like breathing!

But Ismail put him out of his agony. 'We're going to be busy for the next few hours. Until then, you'll stay here, and make no more damned trouble for us. After that, I couldn't care less what happens to you.' Slightly relieved, but still apprehensive, Iago half rose from the chair.

Joe grabbed his thin shoulder and crushed him back on to the seat. 'Siddown and shurrup!' he grated. Then he looked at Tiger. 'Leave him here? Think that's safe? What if he's right about the fuzz being behind him. They might come back with a warrant after this afternoon's performance.'

Ismail fiddled with his nail file, but didn't use it – a sure sign of his inner worries. 'You may be right – but not because the police are following him.' He looked expressionlessly at Iago. 'You were just having a little fun on your own, weren't you … the coppers think you're a nut.' Iago opened his mouth, but no one was going to listen to him. 'I think we'll take you with us. You're cracked enough to do something crazy and we don't want to get Uncle Ahmed mixed up in this – he doesn't know what goes on upstairs here.' He gave a wink to Joe out of sight of Iago's view, a subtle bit of propaganda for Price to take to the police in due course.

'What we going to do then – take him on the job with us?' Joe sounded incredulous.

'Tie him up, leave him in the car … we can dump him somewhere when we've finished.'

Archie Vaughan came back into the room, with Kalvos close behind, dangling the empty tape spool in his fingers.

'Nobody else next door, Tiger,' reported Vaughan. 'I cracked the back door and went through the place … nothing there except where he climbed up the loft.'

Ismail nodded and looked at his watch. 'A couple of hours before we need start getting organized.' He looked intently at Iago. 'Listen, mister ... you be a good boy and you won't get hurt. Joe, you stay with him here and see that he behaves. I'm going to have an hour's kip. You others can do what the hell you like, as long as you stay stone cold sober. Be back here at eleven – got it?'

The city was quiet at midnight.

The rain had stopped, but the streets were still wet. The pavements glistened under the yellow light of the sodium lamps, as a solitary policeman went on his rounds of Castle Street.

The late night traffic was still quite brisk, but there were few pedestrians about. The public houses were long since closed, there were no big dances on a Monday night and the late cinemas and restaurants were mainly at the other end of town.

The helmeted PC trod his measured steps from shop to shop, flashing a light in the deeper doorways. He hardly expected to find anything – even drunks were a rarity in Cardiff these days. The most he might come across would be a cuddling couple with more than the usual stamina.

There was nothing by the time he reached the Angel Hotel – the end of his beat, just opposite the County Cricket Ground at the Arms Park. He stopped and looked across for a moment at the imposing mass of the castle, which formed the whole of the opposite side of the street, stretching away to Kingsway. The gilt hands of the clock on its ornate tower were just past midnight and the constable thought of his approaching 'refreshment period' back in the Central station.

He ambled back past the broad front of David Powell's department store and jumped slightly when a time switch suddenly extinguished all the window lights.

The main entrance was firmly sealed by a steel grille across the steps. There were four or five other entrances, as the shop ran back through the full thickness of the block to the next street, as well as enveloping two covered arcades which connected the two streets. He had checked those doors on the way up and had had a word with one of the two nightwatchmen, who was putting out his empty milk bottles.

As the slow clop of the police boots faded into the distance, a small door opened cautiously just inside the eastern arcade. A face peeped warily out through the crack.

Betty had been thrown a little, by the appearance of the 'copper', but her timetable was not seriously affected. She had been cooped up in 'Inexpensive Dresses' since six o'clock, and it seemed more like six weeks than six hours.

The regular visits of the caretakers had been no more than a bore – they never looked in the changing cubicles, as she had discovered during her week's employment there.

She had arranged with Tiger Ismail to open the door of the staff entrance at exactly midnight … that was when the watchmen made one of their many cups of tea.

Betty looked out now to see if any of the mob was in Castle Street or sheltering under the castle gate opposite. It had started to drizzle again, giving a good excuse for someone to loiter in a sheltered nook. There was at least another five or ten minutes before the watchmen might start their rounds again – she had stayed all last night as a 'dry run', to get used to their routine.

Another four minutes went by without a sign of anyone and she started to worry. Suddenly, something touched her hand, which was on the edge of the door. Only by a miracle did she avoid squealing with fright. Tiger peered in at her from the gloom of the arcade.

'All OK?' he whispered.

She glared at him. 'Christ, where did you spring from – I thought you were going to be in the street. You frightened the bloody life out of me!'

'I came down the arcade – but damn that, let's get inside.'

She led him rapidly and silently past the clocking-in racks to the staff cloakrooms and they went into the 'Ladies' for a whispered conference.

'The watchmen never come in here,' she explained, 'not even in the night.' Her hard good looks were lost on Tiger. To him, she was just another of the gang – one of the most reliable and efficient members.

'What about the money – that still here?' This was the most important thing; without that they might as well go home.

She nodded quickly. 'I would have rung you if it wasn't … something else, too. They've had a lot more in the jewellery line for Christmas. Not fabulous, but a lot of stuff worth twenty to thirty pounds a time. There must be a thousand quid's worth of stock there, at least – all small things.'

His eyes glistened in the poor light. For some reason, baubles interested him as much as money. One of his ambitions was to have been a big diamond thief, but it was too risky.

'What sort of stuff is it?' he demanded.

'Rings, brooches, costume jewellery … mostly semi-precious, but a few small good stones. Lot of silver, too, but that's a bit bulky.'

'Where is it?'

'Special little department off the Ladies Fashion … there's a safe there, but it came out of Noah's bloody ark. Nikos could crack it with his eyes shut!'

Tiger weighed up the prospects against the risks … that was the way he stayed out of prison.

'Let's go and have a look at it first,' he said.

She put a hand on his arm. 'The night men – they keep a pretty sharp eye on it. Their cubbyhole is within sight of the jewellery, that's why they haven't bothered with much of a safe, I suppose.'

Ismail frowned into the dark. 'You mean we've got to knock over the guards before we can collect?'

She nodded. 'Unless you can work fast enough to do it while they're on their rounds. They only stay away about ten minutes at a time, they keep coming back to meet at their little room. Those buggers drink more tea than Joe does beer. If one doesn't turn up, the other has got strict orders to ring the police.' Tiger looked admiringly at her. 'You've sure done your homework, kid.'

She nodded. 'I know – and I can tell you that there's a direct alarm from that cubbyhole to the police station. Just press a button and the balloon goes up!'

Tiger was thinking hard. 'Is it worth the extra risk of nobbling the watchmen?' he mused.

Betty said she thought it was. 'We don't know how long Nikos will be, cracking the big safe in Accounts,' she whispered. 'If he has to blow it, those chaps will come running anyway – after pressing the alarm. If they're out of the way from the start, you can spend all night looting the place.'

He had another deep think, weighing up all the 'pros and cons'. Then he nodded. 'You're right, girl … now listen.'

He outlined the various disasters that had recently happened and explained that they were all making a run for it directly after the job. 'You're all right, Betty,' he ended. 'The coppers don't know you from Adam – or Eve. You can sit tight if you want to … I'd keep on coming to work if I were you, or they'll get suspicious.'

She shook her head. 'I'm going with Joe,' she said firmly. 'Where is he, anyway?'

'Cruising around … I'll go out and flag him down when we decide how to go about things.'

They spent a few minutes drawing up a plan of campaign,

then Ismail glided off into the darkness. He had the knack of moving like the cat that he so often resembled.

A few moments later he was back with Joe Davies and Nikos Kalvos. Joe took a few seconds off to run his hands enthusiastically over Betty's body in the darkness, then they were back to business. She bolted the staff door behind them as soon as they were all inside.

'Where will the nightwatchmen be by now?' breathed Tiger.

She shrugged. 'I've lost track of them, messing about here – you'll have to go looking for them, or catch them as they get back to their den … but mind they don't get a finger to that flaming alarm!'

Tiger padded away, with the other two behind him. Following Betty's directions, they passed through two furniture departments which were joined by arched doorways. They kept a sharp eye and ear for the guards, but there was no sign of them.

A few dim electric bulbs glowed at strategic points, usually where the paths through the various departments crossed. There were a multitude of large displays and deep shadows in which to shelter.

'Could hide a bleeding army in here,' whispered Joe Davies, but Tiger poked him violently as a signal to shut his mouth.

Beyond Carpets and Soft Furnishings, they came across a modern piece of shopfitting which was completely closed by metal grilles and plate glass. The faint light showed displays of jewellery and ornaments, with many gaps where the more expensive items had been removed to the safe for the night.

Tiger held out an arm to stop the others, then pointed ahead to the next corner.

The clink of cups and the muted buzz of conversation came to them from an oversize sentry box made of hardboard, which nestled in a corner.

The Arab pushed the others into the shelter of some fabric displays, then put his mouth close to their ears. 'Get 'em separately after they split up.'

A few moments later, the door of the cubicle opened and a rather fat man came out. He stretched himself, scratched his armpit and set off in the opposite direction, waving a large torch in one hand.

Tiger cursed.

He could not go after this one until the other appeared – if only the first man had come this way.

In a moment, another younger man appeared and moved briskly in their direction.

Tiger nudged Joe as he approached.

As the watchman passed their hideout, Davies leapt out and pinioned him, one big arm around his face and the other gripping his right wrist. Nikos was close behind and grabbed the other arm, kicking his legs from under him at the same time.

The caretaker made no attempt to struggle – he seemed shocked into paralysis.

'The plaster, Nikos,' snapped Tiger, and in a moment the man they had attacked was trussed with wide surgical tape around his ankles and wrists – the strong, adhesive cloth was far better than any string or ropes. Nikos slapped a generous length across the man's face, completely covering the mouth.

'Leave his nose free, for God's sake,' muttered Tiger. 'We don't want another accident.'

Within thirty seconds the watchman was immobilized and silenced. A few more seconds and he was laid out of sight behind the nearest counter.

'Next, please,' said Joe, with facetious glee. They all went after the other man and inside three minutes he had suffered the same ignominious treatment as the first. He managed to cry out as Joe grabbed him but, as there was no one to hear, it didn't matter.

Betty Thomas had kept out of the way during the combat, not from any feminine squeamishness, but from reluctance to be recognized unnecessarily – like Tiger, caution was her strong point. She came up now, after the two watchmen had been hidden out of sight.

'The dispatch room is this way,' she said, leading them to a set of swing doors. Downstairs in the basement was a large packing department leading to a loading bay where Powell's vans were parked for the night. This adjoined a ramp leading up into the back street behind the store, sealed off from it by a wide metal shutter.

Joe opened a small access door in this and stepped cautiously out into the open. Padding up to the street, he made sure that the coast was clear, then came back to help Nikos wind up the steel roller gate. It rumbled with nerve-rending loudness in the still night and as soon as it was high enough to walk under, they left it.

Tiger walked out into the road and cautiously waved down the street.

Archie Vaughan was parked in High Street, a long distance off, but in a position where he had a clear view down the back street behind Powell's. As soon as he saw the signal, he slid Ismail's Ford along and turned without hesitation down the ramp and into the loading bay between the lorries. Tiger padded inside and there was another excruciating minute as they wound the door down again.

'Is he all right?' demanded Ismail, peering through the back window of the car.

Archie leaned over the seat and looked down to where Iago Price lay trussed and taped like a turkey. 'Seems OK – still breathing. At least, his eyes are still rolling around,' he remarked callously.

'Better get him out and dump him in the office – put those two other characters in there with him.'

They collected the three bound figures and lay them on the floor of the caretakers' cubicle.

'Right, they can't come to any harm there,' snapped Tiger. 'Let's get on with the job.'

Outside, he whispered to Betty, 'Keep an eye on those fellers through the crack in the door. You needn't let them see you, but if they try to get loose or get to that alarm button, go in there and kick them around a bit … OK?'

Tiger and the Greek made for the Accounts office, which was on the second floor, while Archie and Joe Davies started on the Jewellery department. They had to burst open the shuttering first, using a mixed collection of housebreaking tools brought from the car.

Upstairs, Nikos Kalvos was scratching his head over the safe. 'I don't know if I can tickle it open, Tiger … I'll give it a few goes, then I'll have to blast it.' Tiger scowled at him. "You're always yakking about what a marvellous bloody cracksman you were back in Greece … so get on and prove it! I'll give you half an hour, then we use the "jelly".'

After fifteen minutes Nikos was sweating like a pig, but still fiddling with the combination lock without success. All he had managed to do was to put the alarm system out of action, but was no further forward towards getting the door open.

Joe came up from the ground floor to interrupt Ismail's rising impatience.

'We've busted the door and carried some of the silver and good-looking stuff to the car, but we'll need Nikos to open the safe. It's only a glorified tin box, but that's where the best stuff will be.'

Tiger looked angrily at his watch. 'Ten minutes – then he'll come down and open it for you … if he can, which I doubt! After that, we blow this thing and to hell with the noise.'

He kicked the big safe viciously, showing a rare display of feeling. Joe went away and left a perspiring Nikos to carry on with his stethoscope and fingertips.

He was destined never to see the inside of that particular safe.

Meredith dreamed that he was back in the Army, a provost-sergeant crouched in a shelled-out building on the wrong side of the Rhine. A shell came whistling down at him and as it got nearer, the whine changed into a frightening clamour.

He groped his way out of the dream to find his bedside telephone ringing. His wife, immunized by years of bells ringing in the night, slept on undisturbed as he mumbled groggily into the instrument.

'Ellis here, sir .... can you come in at once. I think we've got 'em!' His voice was alert and bursting with delight. Some of it rubbed off on to Meredith as he shook off the last mists of sleep.

'What's up? Where are you?'

'Headquarters ... I was already here questioning a couple of thieves we caught red-handed in the Co-op. But that can wait! A minute ago we had a call from a nightwatchman in an office block that faces the back entrance of David Powell's department store in Castle Street. He was looking out of a window and saw a car going into Powell's loading bay. A chap was directing it in, looked a bit fishy, so he made a nine-nine-nine.'

Meredith scowled in the darkness of his bedroom. 'So why ring me ... the Pandas and mobiles can deal with it, can't they?'

Ellis was fond of leaving the punchline to the very end.

'This watchman – he was smart enough to give us the number of the car. Information Room had it on their special list ... it's Tiger Ismail's Ford!'

Meredith leapt out of bed, still hanging on to the phone.

'Get that place sealed off – everything on wheels around it! I'll skin anybody who lets them get out! I'll be there in ten minutes.'

Nine minutes later, Old Nick skidded to a halt outside Police Headquarters, picked up Ellis from the steps and accelerated off into the one-way system that led them back to the castle.

'What's been happening?' he demanded as the car slithered around a bend on the rain-soaked road.

'I've got three patrol cars and a Panda around the block and four extra men sent down from Central – that's eleven men strung out all around the building. There are umpteen doors – in the arcades as well – but that should bottle them up. One of the Pandas is parked across the loading bay entrance, so they can't get their car out now.'

Meredith nodded his satisfaction as they ran across a red light at a deserted intersection.

'Any sign that they've heard us coming?'

Bob Ellis shook his head. 'Not a peep – the place looks as dead as a doornail, so the mobiles reported on the air just now. They're just standing to, not making any attempt to get in until we arrive.'

'Any watchmen in that place?'

'Two – nothing heard of them tonight. There's an alarm system from their cabin to Central, but it hasn't gone off.'

Meredith slowed down as he came level with the first tower of the great castle. A few yards further and he stopped behind a black police Wolseley parked at the kerb.

A uniformed patrolman stepped from the shadows of the arcade and touched his cap.

'Nothing happened so far, sir … all the doors seem secure.'

Meredith stepped back and looked along the dimly lit arcade.

'Like a bloody rabbit warren! Does all that balcony belong to the shop?' He pointed to an upper veranda where an ornate Victorian railing ran at first-floor level for the full length of the arcade.

'Yessir – there's a couple of bridges across to the

premises opposite. All the doors should be locked, but it'll take a lot of men to seal it off properly.'

Old Nick looked along the Castle Street frontage of the store.

'How many of them inside, d'you know?'

'Only two were seen, sir, the driver and the chap who let them in. If it is Ismail, I suppose he'll have his three yobs with him,' replied Ellis.

A movement in the gloom along the street caught Meredith's eye. Another constable was standing guard over the main entrance.

'Well, no good standing here scratching ourselves,' he muttered. 'What's the best way in?'

The patrolman, a sergeant, jerked a thumb down the arcade.

'Until we get someone to come from the firm with keys, the best bet is the little staff entrance down there. Make a hell of a row, though, smashing it open!'

They moved towards the door in the arcade. As they padded along, a flashing light flickered urgently from the other end, where the tunnel joined the street at the back.

'I'll get it,' murmured Ellis. He was wearing crêpe-soled shoes and sped soundlessly down to the light, which was being waved by a constable from the Panda car.

A moment later he was back at Meredith's side, slightly out of breath. 'Information Room – the alarm has just gone off from inside. They telephoned the shop number, but there was no reply … the phone is switched through to the watchmen's cabin at night.'

Meredith straightened up and stopped whispering. 'Right, no need for all this cloak-and-dagger stuff now. Let's get in there!' As he made for the door, he snapped some instructions at the sergeant. 'Get on the air and ask for more men … any men, get 'em off their backsides in the canteen. And any other cars that are free … and tell them to roust out the management of this place, someone who knows the geography and has a full set of keys. This might be a long job … better tell the Chief what's going on too, for good measure.'

The sergeant ran off, his boots shattering the still night air.

Meredith shone his torch on the door. 'Good lock – take some breaking open.'

He and Ellis threw their weight against the door without making the slightest impression. They waited for the brawny patrol sergeant to come back and add his weight, but still the door showed no signs of giving way.

'The – fanlight – you're the smallest, Ellis,' snapped Meredith.

'Thanks very much!' muttered the five-foot-ten inspector.

The other two lifted him on their hands and he was able to tear off the wire-mesh grille by sheer brute force.

With the butt end of the sergeant's torch he smashed out all the glass, then was ignominiously pushed through to fall heavily and painfully amongst the fragments of glass on the other side.

Bleeding from several small cuts and cursing fluently in a mixture of English and Welsh, Ellis opened the door and let them in. As he did so, another car pulled up at the Castle Street end of the arcade and five policemen tumbled out, two of them plainclothes CID men on the night shift.

'One of you stay on this door,' snapped Meredith. 'Lock it and yell like hell if anyone tries to get out.'

He plunged off into the darkness, the white edge of his pyjama trousers flapping below his turn-ups.

When he reached the first showroom he split the party into three groups. 'Turn on all the light switches you can find.' He groped around the staircase at the end of the room and flooded the area with light. 'That's a start … now get going and if you meet these villains blow your whistles so that we know where you are – this place is like a maze.'

Two men ran up the wide stairs and three more took the right hand corridor which ran between acres of furniture.

'Ellis, let's try this way.'

The two senior men went off at a trot, flashing their torches in search of more light switches. As they turned the next bend, a drumming noise came eerily through the deserted store.

'What the devil's that?' demanded Old Nick. Ellis broke into a run and at the end of the alleyway saw light streaming from a crack in a doorway.

'Somebody in there, sir … what the bloody hell!'

As he spoke, the door crashed open and in the patch of brightness that flooded out, a weird figure tottered across the carpet. It swayed and tottered then fell full- length on to the floor.

'Looks like a flaming Egyptian mummy!' croaked the imaginative Ellis. He dashed the last few yards at Olympic sprint standard and stood over the wriggling body as Meredith caught up.

The policemen knelt down and tore off the sticking plaster from the man's mouth – a painful process, judging by the look of agony on his face.

The face was that of Iago Price.

'You again! … what in God's name are you doing here?' Meredith's amazement was almost comical, but no one was in a laughing mood.

'Two more inside,' gasped Iago, his face deathly pale except for the angry red streaks where the plaster had been. His moustache had been half pulled out and he felt sick and frightened.

Ellis dashed into the cubicle and began to un-gag the two nightwatchmen, while Meredith unwrapped the surgical tape from Iago's wrists and ankles.

'Who did this – how many are on the premises?' he asked in a steely voice.

'Ismail – and that long-haired chap,' quavered Iago. 'And an Italian or something, as well as the little fellow who was in the pub. There's a girl as well … blast her!'

Ellis came back out of the cabin. 'The men are all right – just leave 'em a minute till their circulation comes back.'

Meredith was more concerned about the location of the thieves.

'Price, where are they, d'you know?'

Iago sat up painfully, rubbing his wrists. He waved feebly across at the ransacked jewellery shop. 'They were looting that place, until they heard you banging on the door. Then they ran upstairs to the offices … they're going to blow the safe – the others are up there.'

Old Nick looked fiercely at Ellis. 'Have you got a whistle?'

The inspector shook his head. It was years since he'd blown one.

A voice came weakly from the cubicle. 'There's one on the shelf here – I always kept it handy,' said the elder of the two caretakers.

Ellis found the whistle and began blowing it again and again.

Meredith went into the cubbyhole to see the other men.

'As soon as you're all right, I'd like you to help us … you know the way around. Can you open one of the rear doors to let in more officers?'

One of the watchmen stumbled across with Meredith and opened a door leading on to the back street, letting in three constables who were banging on the door, trying to answer the summons of the police whistle.

'Lock it again and one of you stand guard here,' snapped Old Nick. He hurried back to the cubicle and spoke to Iago. 'I'll talk to you later … but who set off the alarm?'

'I did!' answered the amateur sleuth proudly, 'I

managed to get up and lean against it until that blasted woman came in and kicked me back to the floor!'

The motor patrol sergeant came back with two other men and they all set out for the upstairs accounts office, leaving Iago alone to nurse his bruises. In the office on the second floor, the five intruders listened to the distant police whistle with varying shades of apprehension.

The alarm had gone off a moment before, in spite of Betty's watchfulness ... they had abandoned the jewellery shop and raced up to Tiger to see what he was going to do.

His plan was simple – drop everything and get out.

Archie Vaughan was wringing his hands in anguish and already counting the years he would spend 'over the wall' as a result of tonight's fiasco.

'How the 'ell did they get on to us?' he moaned.

'That flaming private eye!' snarled Betty. 'I wish I'd kicked his head off now.'

'Couldn't have been him – the law was here straight after the alarm went off ... they must have been tipped off some other way.' Joe Davies sounded almost elated at the prospect of the coming battle.

Tiger smacked the office desk with the flat of his hand. 'Shurrup, all of you ... what are we goin' to do ... stick together or separate?' He went to the door and listened intently. The safe still stood intact in its corner, with Nikos' preparations for blasting the door still half finished. On the table, five suitcases – stolen from the store – stood open and pathetically empty, waiting for the cash.

'What about the car – can we try a run for it,' hissed Archie, his eyeballs rolling in fear.

'Don't be bloody stupid ... they'll have blocked the gate by now. We'll have to split up ... the store is big enough to lose an army in – if we play it clever, we can slip out somewhere. They'll have the rozzers on the doors, but there's plenty of windows.'

Joe Davies had an idea – a typically violent, destructive

idea. 'What about a diversion, Tiger … we could start a good old fire. That'll draw 'em off for a bit.'

Ismail nodded. He was as pale as his dark colour allowed, but calm and still calculating the odds with mechanical precision.

'We'll split up now … all make your own way – and the best of luck. Joe and Nikos can find something that'll burn, to pull off the bobbies while we scatter. Betty – you first … get lost, girl!'

She slipped reluctantly out of the false shelter of the office, followed by Archie Vaughan. Joe and the Greek went next, leaving Tiger alone.

He went quickly to the case in which they had brought the gelignite and took out a handful of rings and brooches. He had palmed these from the loot taken from the jewellery store when they were taking it all to the car. The rest of the stuff was now lying uselessly in the boot, but Tiger had creamed off the better stuff for himself. It was a poor substitute for the expected cash haul, but better than nothing in the disastrous circumstances.

He crammed them into his pocket and slipped out into the darkness of the store. The fur department was immediately outside and he found time to regret leaving all the mink that hung on the racks nearby. As he slipped like a shadow towards the stairs, a muffled roar and a blast of hot air signalled the start of the diversion on the floor below.

Joe Davis and Nikos had found the decorating department and some shelves of turpentine substitute. Within seconds, they had hurled dozens of bottles at the racks of wallpaper and paint … one touch of Nikos' cigarette lighter had converted the place into an inferno.

The Greek had to run to avoid being roasted – when he slowed down, he found he was on his own.

But not for long … as he trod on the first tread of the staircase, a pair of massive hands grabbed him by the shoulders and two more hands snapped handcuffs on his wrists. Two constables from a motor patrol smiled happily at each other from behind his back.

'One down and four to go! … hope someone has called the fire brigade, or there'll be smoked Tiger for breakfast!'

Betty Thomas had not lasted long, either.

Knowing the layout of the store fairly well, she managed to reach the basement by various obscure routes. She had a vague idea of hiding in a delivery van until morning, but as she entered the loading bay, a tall detective stepped from behind a pile of boxes and grabbed her wrist.

She fought, kicked and bit him, but the officer seemed impervious and eventually she subsided into weeping, hysterical frustration. A uniformed constable appeared from somewhere and the plainclothes man grinned at him. 'Get on your Noddy set, Jack, and ask Central to send a woman PC over pronto … before I fall in love with Spitting Susie here!'

Archie Vaughan was next for the chop. He saw his enemies coming at a distance, but it did him no good. As he entered the electrical department, two blue-mackintoshed figures appeared at the other end. He turned and fled, but after two corners along the passageway, he found himself facing a wall of flame from the hardware section. There was no side turning and he had to stand helplessly and even walk into the arms of the approaching constables as the flames drove him back.

He went meekly enough, which was more than could be said for Joseph Stalin Davies.

Leaving the office, Joe had got down to the ground floor unobserved but while working his way around to the front entrance, he had heard voices and saw flashing torches coming towards him. He ducked under the nearest counter and lay doggo amongst boxes of nylons and ladies underwear while two policemen went past. The shop lights came on, their brilliance nearly blinding him, but no one came near.

He thought he had got away with it when two new voices approached.

'We'll have to start combing the place from end to end, Ellis.' Meredith had come into the ground floor main hall from the opposite end to the inspector, who had a uniformed constable with him.

'There are a dozen salesrooms the size of this, sir – take half the police force to box them in!'

'Then we'll have to use half the police force,' snapped Old Nick. 'There are two of them still on the loose – the most important two!'

'Where are we going to start, sir … the fire brigade have just moved in, they're crawling all over the first floor. They say it'll be easy to get under control, but they've got a couple of doors open for hoses and extinguishers and that … we don't want to lose our friends through there!'

Joe pricked up his ears. The added confusion of firemen tramping through the store might be his salvation.

He had to work fast, as Meredith was starting to comb the salesroom already. 'We'll work from the front entrance inwards … call some more men and let's get this place checked out.'

Davies waited no longer … doubled up, he ran behind the row of display cases along the wall, dashing past the occasional openings, trusting to luck that no one was looking for the split second he needed to pass each gap.

His luck held until he got to the end of the row.

Then he had to dodge around a corner with no cover, in order to get into the next sales area.

Though his feet made no sound on the thick carpets, Bob Ellis saw something move from the corner of his eye.

'Hey – you! Sir, there's one of 'em – around that

corner!' As he bellowed, he started running and four heavy pairs of feet were soon pounding after Joe Davies, who had about fifteen yards' start.

Ellis still had the police whistle and he blew it as he ran, shrilling an alarm through the ground floor.

The next department was Menswear and at the end was a narrow passage leading on to some changing rooms.

As he neared it, Joe suddenly swerved as he saw two uniformed men appear in the gloom. The only other way was down a staircase to the basement. He went down six steps at a time and hammered away along the centre aisle.

Though he was no coward, the continuous pursuit was telling on him and he was working up a state of panic. He turned several corners aimlessly, having no plan of escape except blind flight.

There appeared to be no other stairs going up and in a few seconds Davies found himself actually running back towards his pursuers. Meredith and a mobile sergeant suddenly appeared right in front of him. They dropped to a crouch as they blocked the alleyway ahead of him. He skidded round and found himself facing Ellis and a constable.

Cornered, he acted just like the animal that was never far beneath his swarthy skin. His mouth pulled back to expose teeth bared in a desperate grin of defiance as he looked about him for a weapon. There were plenty to be had, as they were in the kitchenware department. Prominent amongst the wares displayed nearby were kitchen knives of all shapes and sizes.

He leapt to the nearest shelf and grabbed a wicked-looking meat knife with a riveted wooden handle and an eight-inch razor-edged blade.

'Right, coppers … come and get me!' he screeched, his eyes glaring like organ stops and spittle flecking the corners of his mouth.

'Drop that, Davies,' cracked out Meredith. 'There are

about twenty of us in the store … you'll only be done for theft as it is … don't add manslaughter or GBH to it, for God's sake!'

'Get stuffed!' screamed Joe, hysterically. 'You're going to do me for that Rourke job, ain't you … so what I gotta lose?'

He stood half-crouched in the passage between the shelves, the knife point waving ominously from side to side.

The constable with Ellis began moving ponderously towards the cornered man. He was a great ugly fellow, apparently quite without fear. He seemed quite prepared to fall on Joe, knife or no knife.

'Get back, will you!' snapped Meredith. 'He's not worth getting injured for … he can't get away, so don't let's have any heroics.'

The PC stopped, looking slightly aggrieved. He was the sort that got most of the medals in wartime – often posthumously.

Davies looked sideways at him, then back at Meredith and the sergeant. 'Can't get out, can I? … You bloody see if I can't, mister!'

He lunged towards Meredith with the knife and the chief superintendent jumped backwards with surprising agility. He was no coward either, but could see no point in getting slit open merely to arrest a man a few moments sooner than was inevitable.

It was Bob Ellis who brought the deadlock to a rapid finish.

Right alongside him were some mincing machines, the sort with a heavy crank handle. They must have weighed at least seven pounds apiece, being made of cast steel.

With a sudden movement, he grabbed one in each hand and hurled them at Joe Davies.

The first one was fended off by an upraised arm, but the second caught Davies on the side of the head with a sickening thud.

Before it had even dropped to the floor, the oversized constable had uttered a bull-like roar and rushed in on Joe. He grabbed his knife arm, paralyzing it so that the weapon fell harmlessly to the ground. The other three officers dashed across to pinion his arms. In spite of the shattering blow on the head, Davies fought like a madman. No one had any handcuffs and a new clothesline from the shelves was pressed into service to truss him up until they could get him to a police van.

'Only Tiger on the loose now,' said Ellis a few moments later, when they had got their breath back and their collars straightened.

'Make sure all those damn doors are shut … Ismail's got more cunning than a bag full of monkeys.'

They went back to the ground floor where firemen and more police were thrashing around. 'This place is getting like the January sales,' he snapped. 'Sergeant, run round all the exits and make sure that there's a man on each … and see if anyone's seen a sign of Ismail.' The sergeant went off at a gallop and Old Nick turned to Ellis. 'We're getting disorganized, Ellis … and I hate it. Now where the hell is Ismail?'

At that moment, Tiger was crouched in the darkness at the back of a window display, at a corner where one of the arcades joined the back street.

He had worked his way around part of the ground floor, hoping to slip out through one of the doors in the confusion created by the arrival of firemen. But policemen rapidly appeared to guard each exit and he sank back into the darkness.

Working his way along the wall behind the elegant displays of the arcade windows, he got to the nearest point to where he would like to break out. There was no door here, but neither was there a police guard.

The windows had plywood screen cutting them off from the shop, but here and there were hinged panels or narrow entrances for the window dressers to get through. He peered through one of these and saw two dummies dressed in cocktail gowns. Beyond these was the plate glass of the window and, in the light of the street lamps, he could see a deserted police car parked at the kerb.

The back street carried on to his left until it joined High Street, which met Castle Street at right angles. Earlier that evening he had left a second car parked in High Street. It was near a couple of casino clubs and late parking would not arouse the suspicions of the nosiest constable. This was part of his private getaway plan, typical of his calculating mind. He had rented an almost new Vauxhall Cresta as an insurance against a major snag … and now he was thanking his stars for his foresight. If only he could get the hundred yards from the store to the car. The keys were in his pocket and if he could get away from the immediate vicinity without the car being identified, he still stood a good chance of slipping clean away.

The problem was getting out of the shop itself … it looked as if there was only one way – through the window.

He crept through the gap in ply screens and crouched between the dummies. There was no one in sight outside and he began looking around cautiously for an implement.

As well as the mannequins, there was a display of evening accessories on a metal stand. This was supported by a metal rod screwed into a heavy cast iron base. He tore off the glittery handbag and gloves and gripped the rod determinedly.

After another glance through the window to make sure that no bobby was standing watching him, he stepped boldly up to the glass and struck it a resounding blow with the metal base. To his dismay nothing happened, apart from a deafening clang and a tingling up his arms.

In desperation, he took the end of the rod in both hands

and swung it high over his shoulder like a golf club.

This time, it did the trick!

There was a minor explosion and a shattering sound like a multiple motorway collision. Most of the window fell out, and after kicking free one large piece at the bottom, he jumped out into the street.

Seconds later, he was racing away up the side street, already feeling for the car keys in his pocket as he ran.

Tiger was just about to congratulate himself on getting clear away when a series of yells and blasts on a police whistle came from the mouth of the arcade.

Without looking around, he hammered around the corner into the brightly lit High Street, praying that no loitering policeman was nearby.

He had fifty yards start from the store and the Vauxhall was now almost in front of him. He threw himself into the driving seat and blessed the engine when it started from cold at the first touch. He was facing down towards the castle and by the time he had covered the few yards to it he was already doing forty-five. The traffic lights at the junction were red, but he hardly noticed, swerving around to the right, accelerating and changing up to top as fast as the big three-litre engine would allow.

Immediately ahead of him was another set of lights where the main east-west and north-south roads of the city intersected. Here a one-way system began and he should have swung left, but the escape route to the east – which meant England and the Continent – was straight on. He hesitated for a fraction of a second, then forged on over the lights, again at red. To turn into the one-way loop would add another quarter of a mile to the escape route and any pursuing police car could cut him off by racing up Queen Street the wrong way, as he was doing now.

So Ismail charged on at sixty-five miles an hour, headlights blazing into the eyes of a succession of astonished late night drivers coming down at him in the proper direction. He tore up the centre of the road, the oncoming vehicles shying away, one actually mounting the pavement in consternation.

His luck held until the far end of the main shopping street, where the one-way system rejoined it again. As he was passing the Capitol Cinema, the sound he had been dreading hit his ears … the hee-haw of a police siren.

He flicked his eyes up to the driving mirror to try to gauge the distance of the police car. This could not have distracted him for more than a quarter of a second, but it was a quarter of a second too much.

A large lorry, carrying a great steel container for industrial waste, came lumbering around the corner from the bypass, right into the path of the Vauxhall. It was only doing about twenty and even after the shock of finding a car almost under his windscreen, the driver was able to pull up within a few yards.

Tiger never actually hit the lorry, but in avoiding it, he pushed the Cresta beyond the limit of its road holding.

The car screeched around in a half circle, all brakes locked and then somersaulted twice. It came to rest on all four wheels on the pavement, its front bumper ironically having smashed in the door of the City Police Social Club a few yards from the cinema.

Seconds later, the patrol car screamed to a raucous halt alongside and the police officers leapt out to help the lorry driver drag Tiger Ismail from the wrecked Vauxhall.

He was unconscious, but otherwise seemed to have hardly a scratch.

The policemen looked at the shattered door of their club and then at the limp body of the fugitive.

'This bugger had it in for us all ways, Dave' muttered the sergeant.

The next day was one for tying up loose ends and picking up the pieces.

‘Poetic justice, that’s what it is!’ said Bob Ellis with obvious satisfaction, as he put the phone down. ‘Ismail’s in the next cubicle to poor old Summers!’

‘What’s the score with them?’ asked Dai Rees.

‘Summers is showing signs of coming back to this world ... the doctors never give you a straight answer, but I think they expect him to start coming round before long. The other swine is all right, just concussion for an hour, but hardly a mark on him. Still, he'll be nice and fit to stand trial.’

Meredith came into the main CID room. He had just been telling the tale to the Chief Constable.

‘Chief sends his compliments,’ he muttered grudgingly. ‘Good night’s work.’

Ellis grinned. ‘Worth a night out of bed to see Joe Davies catch that mincer across the side of his head. Are those four up before the stipe[1] this morning?’

Meredith nodded. ‘Joe needed a stitch in his head, but he’s all right otherwise. Ismail will have to wait a few days, but we’ll get the others remanded out of the way. I don’t know what the DPP will make of the charges. Last night’s party will put them all away for a year or two, but the rest of the business is a bit dicey.’

Ellis tapped angrily on his desk with a pencil. ‘Be a damn shame to see ’em get away with anything. There’s Summers and Terry Rourke to be squared up somehow.’

Old Nick shrugged. ‘If none of them cough, we’ve had it!’ He pulled at a black eyebrow pensively. ‘We haven’t a clue which one of them did what, but I should think we might squeeze enough out of ’em to get them a fair stretch – apart from the girl, she won’t cop much.’

Ellis suddenly grinned, his fair, rosy face lighting up.

‘That Price character – he turns up everywhere. We’d better offer him an honorary appointment on the Force.’

---

[1]Magistrate

Old Nick scowled one of his darkest scowls.

'If he crosses my path again, I'll kick in his other ribs for him. He can't do a thing right. He's lucky not to have ended up like Rourke.'

The same sentiments were being bandied about in the saloon bar of the Glendower Arms. Lewis Evans was propped belligerently behind the bar, glaring at Iago Price.

'What's going to happen about my tape recorder, then? The police have confiscated it as an exhibit, as well as the casing being bust!'

Dilys studied herself intently in the mirror of her compact as she threw in her own drop of acid.

'Right blooming hero, our Iago! Sounds the alarm after the coppers get there! Good job David Powell's don't know that, or they'd take their cheque back again.'

She was busy deflating Iago's ego over the gratitude the store had showered on him that morning. Meredith had mysteriously exaggerated the part Iago had played and the managing director had handed him twenty-five guineas and the promise of all future enquiry business from David Powell's.

'You can sneer, but I earned that tip the hard way,' he said, nettled by their lack of hero-worship. 'That damned woman, Betty, nearly kicked a hole in me after I pressed that button. She must have been wearing stiletto toecaps, not heels.'

Dilys hauled her mascara-laden eyelids up and looked at him. 'You stick to randy husbands and never-never dodgers, chum. You're out of your class with people like Tiger Ismail.'

Lewis nodded solemn agreement.

'How's your leg? Fallen through any more ceilings since yesterday?' he asked evilly, still simmering over his beloved tape recorder.

Iago shot to his feet and forgot to wince with the

alleged pain. 'I'm going to find another pub where the landlord isn't so damn familiar. You coming, Dill?'

'No,' she said calmly. 'And you sit down, you haven't finished the drink I bought you.'

Iago subsided on to his stool and sulked. His face still had red lines across it, his leg was scratched, his chest ached and his moustache was sore, but all he got for his honourable wounds was sarcasm and abuse. But hope sprang eternal and he turned back to the blonde.

'What about coming out with me tonight to celebrate and all that?'

Dilys studied her pink fingernails as if she had just discovered them.

'Sorry, pet, I've got a date already. With a policeman – a real one, with a whistle and all.'

Iago swallowed his drink and slunk away.

The Sixties Mysteries

by

Bernard Knight

The Lately Deceased
The Thread of Evidence
Mistress Murder
Russian Roulette
Policeman's Progress
Tiger at Bay
The Expert

For more information about **Bernard Knight**
and other **Accent Press** titles
please visit

www.accentpress.co.uk

CPSIA information can be obtained
at www.ICGtesting.com
Printed in the USA
LVOW12s2016010916
502845LV00001B/16/P